SASSY SOCIA
BLACK SHEEP

You heard it from [...] first…. Casino magn[...] Blake Fortune has bedded PR assistant Sasha Kilgore and just might be planning to pop the question! But don't break out the bubbly quite yet—a sordid sibling love triangle could be looming.

Not long after Sasha and her handsome boss, Creed Fortune, were spotted dancing cheek to cheek at his brother Case's wedding reception, she was caught getting hot and heavy with Blake Fortune during the grand opening of his newest casino.

Sounds like Blake's stolen Sasha Kilgore right out from under his brother Creed's nose.

[...]g, [...] rumor has it that she's been lusting after Blake since adolescence!) It's a well-known fact that Case and Creed Fortune have been at odds with their wayward half brother, Blake, for years. But who knew that brotherly rivalry would reach such epic proportions? Hmmm…I wonder if poor Sasha is privy to the fact that she's being used as a pawn in this shameless show of macho one-upmanship.

Until next time!

Dear Reader,

Welcome back to the world of the DAKOTA FORTUNES with Kathie DeNosky's *Mistress of Fortune*. In this tale of revenge and subterfuge you'll meet Blake Fortune, the youngest Fortune brother…and the one with the most to prove. For years Blake has felt like an outsider around his family, his life upended by the trouble his mother has created for his father and new stepmother. But when the time comes to test his family loyalties, it's a throw of the dice to see which way Blake will turn.

Next month be sure to pick up Jan Colley's *Expecting a Fortune*. Yes…you've guessed it. The tomboy Fortune is pregnant. But who's the daddy? And what's *her* daddy going to do when he finds out? Anyone for a shotgun wedding?

We hope you are enjoying all of the wonderful stories in the DAKOTA FORTUNE series. Thanks for choosing Silhouette Desire.

Happy Reading,

Melissa Jeglinski

Melissa Jeglinski
Senior Editor
Silhouette Desire

Please address questions and book requests to:
Silhouette Reader Service
U.S.: 3010 Walden Ave., P.O. Box 1325, Buffalo, NY 14269
Canadian: P.O. Box 609, Fort Erie, Ont. L2A 5X3

KATHIE DeNOSKY

MISTRESS
OF
FORTUNE

Published by Silhouette Books
America's Publisher of Contemporary Romance

This book is dedicated to the authors
of the DAKOTA FORTUNES. It was a real pleasure
working with you and I hope we get to do it again soon.

Special thanks and acknowledgment are given to
Kathie DeNosky for her contribution to the
DAKOTA FORTUNES series.

SILHOUETTE BOOKS

ISBN-13: 978-0-373-76789-2
ISBN-10:   0-373-76789-7

MISTRESS OF FORTUNE

Copyright © 2007 by Harlequin Books S.A.

KATHIE DeNOSKY

lives in her native southern Illinois with her husband and one very spoiled Jack Russell terrier. She writes highly sensual stories with a generous amount of humor. Kathie's books have appeared on the Waldenbooks bestseller list and received a Write Touch Readers' Award from WisRWA and a National Readers' Choice Award. She enjoys going to rodeos, traveling to research settings for her books and listening to country music. Readers may contact Kathie at: P.O. Box 2064, Herrin, Illinois 62948-5264 or e-mail her at kathie@kathiedenosky.com.

THE DAKOTA FORTUNES

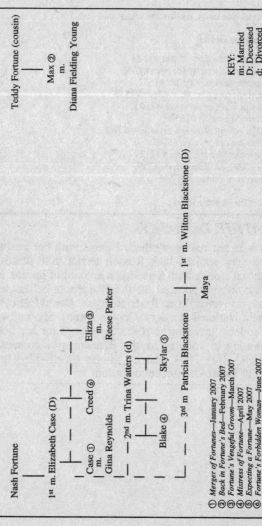

Nash Fortune

1st m. Elizabeth Case (D)

Case ①
m.
Gina Reynolds

Creed ⑥

Eliza ③
m.
Reese Parker

— 2nd m. Trina Watters (d)

Blake ④

Skylar ⑤

— 3rd m Patricia Blackstone — 1st m. Wilton Blackstone (D)

Maya

Teddy Fortune (cousin)

Max ②
m.
Diana Fielding Young

KEY:
m: Married
D: Deceased
d: Divorced

① *Merger of Fortunes*—January 2007
② *Back in Fortune's Bed*—February 2007
③ *Fortune's Vengeful Groom*—March 2007
④ *Mistress of Fortune*—April 2007
⑤ *Expecting a Fortune*—May 2007
⑥ *Fortune's Forbidden Woman*—June 2007

One

"Good morning, this is Sasha Kilgore, public relations assistant."

"Hi, Sasha. Blake Fortune, here."

At the sound of his smooth baritone filtering through the phone into her ear, Sasha's heart skipped a beat and she had to remind herself to breathe. "Hello, Blake. What can I do for you today?"

"I need a favor, Sasha."

Every time he said her name, a tiny little flutter in the pit of her stomach reminded her that she apparently still carried the remnants of a schoolgirl's crush for the youngest of the Fortune men.

"I'll do what I can," she said, hoping she didn't sound too eager. "What do you need?"

"You."

"Me?" Her pulse raced and the room suddenly felt as if it had become a vacuum.

"I know this is late in the game to be asking about something like this, but I'm opening a new casino here in Deadwood toward the end of the month and I need your help coming up with a special PR campaign to kick things off. I want it to run though the summer to attract vacationers."

It was completely ridiculous, but she felt a little disappointed that his call wasn't of a personal nature. "Hotels and the gaming industry aren't exactly my area of expertise."

Why hadn't he consulted his own PR director? Surely he had one. After all, this would be the third casino he'd opened in the past four years and she'd heard through the office grapevine that he'd recently formed his own corporation.

"Come on, sweetheart." His use of the endearment sent a little shiver straight up her spine. "We both know you're one of the best. Otherwise you wouldn't be working for Dakota Fortune."

She felt warm all over from just the sound of his voice. "So now you're going to resort to charm and flattery?"

"Is it working?"

She laughed. "No, but it's nice to hear."

"Tell me you'll help me out here, Sasha," he said, his voice taking on the no-nonsense tone she was used to hearing from him. "My public relations director is out on family medical leave, helping his wife with their new twin girls and I'm up against a wall on this. Fortune's Gold is opening in three weeks."

"I've never seen the place and that makes it extremely difficult to come up with ideas that would work for you," she warned.

"Not a problem. Just set a day and time and I'll send my private jet to pick you up."

"I could probably research your needs on the Internet, then—"

"You'll get a better idea if you see the operation firsthand," he said obstinately.

If there was one thing about the Fortune men that she knew as surely as she knew her own name, it was that they didn't take *no* for an answer.

Sighing, she reached for her electronic planner. "The earliest I could possibly meet with you would be day after tomorrow. Would that be convenient or would the following week be better?"

"Friday's great. I'll be looking forward to seeing you. Plan on spending the weekend here in Deadwood, then we'll fly back to Sioux Falls together on Monday morning."

"That's three days."

"Your math skills are impressive."

"And your persistence is annoying."

His deep chuckle caught her off guard. To her knowledge, she hadn't heard him laugh in years and she'd come to the conclusion that his brothers, Case and Creed, had been right when they'd insisted that Blake didn't have a sense of humor. Apparently, they'd been wrong.

"Come on, Sasha. You'll be able to get an idea of what my clientele experience while they're here. That should help you come up with a more attractive promotional offer. And besides, it'll be a nice little break away from the rat race."

Oh, he was good. He knew just what to say and just how far to lower his voice to make her feel as if it really meant a lot to him for her to spend the weekend working on his promotion campaign.

"I suppose it would be nice to get away for a weekend," she said slowly. "I just wasn't aware that it would take that much time to research what you need and come up with a viable plan."

"I thought since you'll be here, you could go ahead and take a look at my other casinos and give me a fresh perspective on ways to promote those as well." He paused. "But if it's a problem…"

When his voice trailed off, she shook her head at how masterful he was at getting what he wanted. "No, no problem. I should be able to clear my calendar for the weekend." Truth to tell, she didn't have anything planned beyond cleaning her apartment and vegging out in front of the television for a Julia Roberts movie marathon on one of the cable channels.

"Then we're set. I'll have my pilot pick you up at eight on Friday morning. And, Sasha?"

"Yes."

"Thanks."

He made the word sound extremely intimate and caused the fluttering in her stomach to go absolutely berserk. But before she could get her suddenly paralyzed vocal cords to respond, he hung up.

"Who was that?"

She looked up at the sound of the familiar male voice to find Creed Fortune standing in her office doorway, looking extremely suspicious.

"It was your brother Blake," she answered cautiously.

"Half brother," Creed corrected tightly. "What did *he* want?"

It was a well-known fact that although Creed and Blake were brothers, they weren't close. Far from it. At the best of times, they were barely civil and at the worst, openly hostile.

"His PR director is on leave of absence and Blake asked me to help him work up a campaign for the opening of a new casino."

She concentrated on inputting her meeting with Blake into her planner. Why did she feel as if she were being disloyal to Creed? They had never been anything more than good friends.

"Are you going to help him?" From the disapproval in Creed's voice, Sasha could tell that he thought she should have turned Blake down.

She nodded. "I see no reason why I shouldn't help him with the grand opening of his new casino."

"I can give you a damned good reason." Creed shook his head. "The son of a bitch can't be trusted. Hell, I'd trust a rattlesnake before I put any kind of faith in Blake Fortune."

"That's a horrible thing to say about your brother, Creed." Being an only child, she'd always wanted a brother or sister and couldn't understand anyone feeling such antagonism toward their sibling. "Whether you get along with him or not, he's still part of your family."

Creed grunted. "The worst part."

Choosing her words very carefully, Sasha met his piercing gaze head-on. "You're one of my best friends, Creed, and I place a lot of value on that friendship. But don't ask me to choose sides. Whatever grievances you have with Blake are between the two of you. I have nothing to do with it."

His mouth flattened into a straight line a moment before he nodded. "All I'm saying is, watch yourself around him, Sasha. He's just like his mother. Bad news."

Hoping to lighten the moment, she grinned. "He'd probably tell me something similar about you. Now, why don't you go back to your office and do something productive while I get back to work?"

Long after Creed had left her alone, Sasha wondered what could possibly have caused the siblings to be at such odds. The two older Fortune brothers, Case and Creed, made no secret of the fact that they had no use for their younger brother. And from everything she'd seen and heard, the feeling was more than mutual. Blake had even gone so far as to leave Dakota Fortune, the multibillion-dollar corporation their grandfather had founded, to build his own empire in the South Dakota gaming industry. As far as she knew, he still maintained his shares of stock in Dakota Fortune and was a member of the board of directors, but had nothing to do with running the enterprise.

Leaning back in her leather desk chair, she stared at the entry she'd just put into her planner. It appeared the hostilities between the Fortune brothers were escalating and they expected those around them to choose sides in their battle of wills—something she had no intention of doing.

Unfortunately, she wasn't sure how she was going to avoid it. She was good friends with one brother and the other brother had always had the ability to make her feel as if the earth moved whenever he looked her way.

Sighing heavily, she shook her head as she opened the browser on her computer and keyed in a search for casinos in the Deadwood, South Dakota, area. When war broke out between Creed and Blake it could very easily destroy whoever got in the way. She needed to keep that in mind and make sure that she wasn't the one caught in the middle when it all came to a head.

Blake sat in the back of his corporate limo at the small private airfield just outside of Deadwood as he waited for his pilot to taxi his Learjet up to the tarmac. After talking with Sasha, he'd spent the past couple of days working with the contractors and decorators responsible for putting the finishing touches on his newest and most luxurious hotel casino yet.

He was determined to see that Fortune's Gold was the premier place to stay in Deadwood and a welcome addition to his newly formed Fortune Casino Corporation. Along with the Belle of Fortune, his hotel casino decorated like an 1880s riverboat, and the Lucky Fortune, a family friendly establishment where parents could drop off their kids at a supervised indoor playground while they gambled without worry, he would be able to successfully offer something to suit everyone's tastes and needs.

Mentally reviewing what still needed to be done, he concluded that he only had a couple of more details to nail down, then he'd have the rest of the weekend to concentrate on Sasha and his mission. He'd told her the truth about his PR man being on leave of absence because of his wife having a set of twin girls. He had, however, omitted that the man had only taken the time off because Blake had insisted on it. A promotional campaign for Fortune's Gold wasn't the real reason behind his calling Sasha or his wanting her to join him for the weekend in Deadwood.

When Blake had attended his oldest brother

Case's wedding reception back in February, he'd noticed that Sasha had been Creed's date. Then, thinking back on it, Blake remembered seeing her with Creed at several functions and family gatherings over the past year. It was clear there was something going on between the two of them and spoke volumes of how special Sasha was to Creed. Blake knew for a fact that his brother was notorious for never dating the same woman more than a few times before he moved on to his next conquest. But Creed obviously felt differently about Sasha and that was what Blake found more than a little interesting. And quite useful.

Sasha had been a freshman when he'd been a senior in high school. Although they hadn't been friends, Blake had a photography class with the shy auburn-haired girl and could have sworn she'd had a crush on him. To his recollection, they'd never spoken back then, but several times he'd caught her watching him, and when his gaze had locked with her pretty green eyes, Sasha had turned several shades of red and glanced away. But in recent years she'd apparently gotten over her schoolgirl crush and turned her attention toward snaring the middle of the Fortune brothers.

Blake smiled. It was past time he rectified that situation and reclaimed what was rightfully his.

When the pilot brought the jet to a halt several feet from the limo, then lowered the door, Blake got out of the car and walked over to offer Sasha his hand as she descended the built-in steps. The moment her soft, delicate palm touched his, a jolt of electric current zinged straight up his arm.

"It's good to see you again, Sasha," he said, dismissing the sensation as some kind of static electricity.

Once she was standing on the pavement beside him, he pulled her into his arms for a lingering hug. When he felt her slender body shiver against him, he concentrated on keeping his expression passive. No sense giving away his intentions before he had the opportunity to ensure their success.

"Did you have a nice, uneventful flight?"

Stepping back, Blake could tell his familiar manner confused her, just as he'd intended. Good. Throwing her off guard and keeping her there was exactly what he wanted to do.

"Y-yes, the flight was blessedly calm." The slight blush on her porcelain cheeks was an encouraging sign and he was confident his plan was going to go off without the slightest hitch.

"I'm glad. At this time of year, turbulence can be a problem."

The early April sun shone weakly through a

bank of clouds, but did little to take the chill from the stiff breeze ruffling the soft auburn curls that had escaped the tight knot of hair at the back of her head. Turning her toward the limo, Blake slipped his arm around her shoulders on the pretense of shielding her from the wind and motioned for his driver to take care of her small travel case.

"Let's get you into the car before you freeze," he said, ushering her over to the long, black sedan.

She drew her coat a little closer as they walked the short distance. "It is rather chilly."

Once they were comfortably seated inside the warmth of the limousine, it wasn't lost on him that she scooted all the way across the bench seat to the other side. He clearly made her nervous and Blake had a good idea why. There was no doubt in his mind that bastard, Creed, had warned her to be wary of him.

"We'll go on to Fortune's Gold from here," Blake said, deciding that work might get her mind off whatever poison Creed had fed her about him. "Then, after you get an idea of the type of clientele I want to attract, we'll eat lunch at Lucky Fortune, tour that facility and end the day at the Belle of Fortune." He smiled. "The Belle is where you'll be staying this weekend."

"That sounds like an excellent idea." To his

relief, she visibly relaxed and her pretty smile caused an odd feeling to grip the pit of his stomach. "I've been doing some research on Deadwood and your competition. After I tour your casinos, I'll be better able to judge if my ideas will work, but I think I already have a plan in mind that I'm sure will fit your needs."

"Great." He made sure to give her his most encouraging smile as he reached over and took her hand in his. Giving it a gentle squeeze, he added, "We'll discuss your ideas tomorrow morning, then have the rest of the weekend to relax and have fun."

Her smile disappeared immediately and she looked as if she might bolt from the car. "Fun?"

If Blake could have gotten his hands on Creed at that moment, he'd have taken great pleasure in tearing his brother limb from limb. No telling what kind of outright lies and distorted half-truths Creed had told her about him.

"I thought since you're here, you might like to try your hand at some of the gaming tables and tour a museum or two. Deadwood has several dedicated to the town's old west history." Thinking quickly, he added, "It might give you another idea or two for the packages I'd like to offer."

She looked thoughtful a moment before she nodded. "You do have a point. Adding admission to one of the museums as part of a special on room rates and meals would be very nice."

As his driver parked the car under the entryway at Fortune's Gold, Blake opened the door and climbed out of the car, holding out his hand to help Sasha to her feet. "Then it's settled," he said, careful to keep the triumph from his voice. "We'll check out a few of the sites tomorrow, then we can decide on the one that will enhance the deals I'll be offering."

When he escorted her through the front entrance of his soon-to-be open casino, he watched her reaction as she looked around at the opulent decor. He'd spared no expense in re-creating the elegance of a high-end Las Vegas establishment, while still maintaining the relaxed atmosphere Deadwood was known for.

"This is beautiful, Blake." She walked over to touch the cool black marble countertop on the registration desk. "I love your use of black, gold and cream. It's very striking and goes perfectly with the crystal chandeliers."

He hadn't counted on her enthusiasm pleasing him quite so much. "I'm hoping Fortune's Gold will attract some of the high rollers from the midwestern cities who might not have the time to make it to Vegas, but could get away for a couple of days to gamble here."

"I'm sure it will be quite popular as a weekend getaway." She continued across the lobby to descend the two steps leading down into the sunken casino area. She nodded toward a variety of slot machines and gaming tables. "I see you have all of the most popular games and gambling devices."

A loud noise on the far side of the casino, where several men were installing some of the decorative trim work, caused her to jump and Blake realized that she still wasn't completely at ease with him. Maybe if he gave her a moment or two alone to collect herself it would help. Throwing her off guard was one thing, but her being a nervous wreck would be detrimental to his plans.

"If you'll excuse me, I need to find the foreman and check to see that everything is still on schedule." He gave her his most reassuring smile. "I'll only be a few minutes."

"Of course." She motioned toward the gaming tables. "If you don't mind, I'll just wander around here to get a better feel for the place."

After talking briefly with the foreman, Blake retrieved a pass key from the main office, then went to find Sasha. When he spotted her, she was standing beside one of the many rows of slot machines and he couldn't help but notice how attractive she was. In high school, she'd been nice looking, but that had only been a hint of things to come. The pretty teenage girl had grown into a strikingly beautiful woman with a figure that could tempt the most pious of saints.

"Is everything still on target for your grand opening?" she asked, clearly disconcerted when she caught him studying her.

"So far, so good." Walking over to her, he placed his hand to the small of her back and guided her toward the elevators. "Ready to see the rooms?"

She stopped to give him a dubious look. "Is that necessary?"

He shrugged. "I thought it might give you a couple of ideas about accommodations for the package offers. I was thinking we could offer about three different options for our guests to choose from."

Looking a little uncertain, she finally smiled. "I told you, the hotel and gaming industry isn't my area of expertise. But touring the rooms does sound like an excellent idea and might help me make the offers more attractive for guests to bring spouses and children."

"PR is PR, whether it's for a casino or a corporation like Dakota Fortune," he said, stepping back for her to enter the elevator. "It's just a different market."

When the doors whispered shut, she laughed

and shook her head. "There's a little more to it than that, Blake."

Her soft voice saying his name did strange things to his insides, but he didn't give it a second thought. He was on a mission, and the success or failure of his objective depended on him keeping a cool head and not letting emotion enter into the equation. It was the way he did business and it had served him quite well over the past four years.

When the elevator doors swished open on the top floor, Blake guided Sasha down a short hall to the executive suites. He'd known in advance which one he'd be showing her and made sure the housekeeping staff had it ready for her inspection.

"This is one of the suites we'll be offering to the whales."

"Whales?"

Fitting the key card into the lock, he opened the door when the light blinked green. "That's the term used in the gaming industry for high rollers. They expect to get their rooms and meals free because they drop more than enough money in the casino to cover the costs, as well as make us a nice profit."

"In other words, it's incentive to get them to gamble in your establishment," she said, glancing around at the expertly decorated rooms.

"That's the idea," he said, nodding. "With

enough comps, they'll be happy to stay here and gamble exclusively with us instead of visiting the other casinos."

She walked slowly around the suite's living room. "This looks like something I might see on one of the television shows about Las Vegas." Turning to face him, she smiled approvingly. "I would think your whales will be quite pleased with this kind of complimentary service."

Nodding, Blake walked over to open the French doors leading to the bedroom. "That's what I'm aiming for. I want this to be *the* hotel for the wealthy when they visit Deadwood."

"I haven't seen the other hotels in town, but I think you've accomplished your goal. This is absolutely beautiful," she said, wandering into the master bathroom. She stopped suddenly and her face reflected her astonishment. "Good lord, Blake. That tub is almost large enough to swim laps." She shook her head. "I don't think I've ever seen a bathtub that large."

Walking up behind her, he placed his hands on her shoulders as they gazed down into the black marble Jacuzzi tub. "We'll offer champagne and caviar for two, in case a gentleman and his lady want an intimate bath together."

Her slender frame stiffened beneath his palms

and she quickly stepped away from him. But not before he felt a slight tremor course through her and noticed a faraway expression cross her face.

"I—I think I've seen enough to know what you'll be offering in the way of accommodations to your wealthier clientele," she said, her steps purposeful as she started for the door. "Why don't we take a look at the standard rooms?"

As he followed her across the living room, Blake smiled. Sasha was nervous all right, but in a good way. He'd bet a day's take in one of his casinos that her reaction to his touch had more to do with the fact that she was still attracted to him than from anything Creed could have told her.

When he pulled the door to the Executive Suite shut behind him, Blake watched the gentle sway of her hips as she walked down the hall to the elevator. He smiled. His plan was not only going to work beautifully, it was going to be a pleasure for both of them.

He was going to seduce Sasha right out from under Creed's nose. And there wasn't a damned thing his older brother could do to stop him.

Two

By the time Blake's driver delivered them to the entrance of the Belle of Fortune Hotel and Casino that evening, Sasha wondered what on earth she'd been thinking when she'd agreed to help him. Spending the day with him had played havoc with her equilibrium and only confirmed what she suspected after she'd talked to him earlier in the week. She was still attracted to him and, although it wasn't the same as when she'd had a crush on him in high school, the fascination was still there just the same. Trying to deny it would be utterly futile.

Unfortunately, he hadn't helped her predicament. From the moment she stepped off his private jet, it seemed as if he'd seized every available opportunity to touch her. Then, there was the matter of his leaning close whenever he spoke to her. It wasn't what he said that caused her to have a perpetual case of goose bumps shimmering over her arms, it was the way he said it. Listening to his smooth baritone as he explained his plans for building a gambling empire, his voice seemed to wrap around her like a warm cocoon. She wasn't sure how he did it, but Blake had managed to make the most mundane detail sound incredibly intimate.

As they walked across the lobby of the authentically decorated hotel, she wondered what had gotten into her. She wasn't that same starry-eyed teenager with a huge crush on the best-looking boy in school. She was a grown woman with a much broader perspective of what to look for in a man besides a handsome face.

It was true that Blake had grown into a devastatingly handsome man who could turn the head of any female possessing a pulse. With his dark-blond hair, blue eyes and sensual good looks, he could just as easily have been a movie star as a businessman.

But it wasn't just the way he looked that caught Sasha's attention. It was his commanding presence that demanded respect and the undivided attention of whomever he was addressing that made him seem larger than life. And if he was smart, he'd use that to his advantage in his promotional campaign.

"Blake, what kind of advertising budget are you planning for the opening of Fortune's Gold?" she asked thoughtfully as they waited for the elevator.

"I haven't set a limit," he said, stepping back for her to enter the car ahead of him. "I'll spend whatever it takes to kick this off the right way. Why?"

"Do you think that's wise, not setting a budget?" she asked.

Pushing the button for the top floor, he shrugged his wide shoulders and shook his head. "Money isn't an issue."

She chided herself for asking such a stupid question. Of course money wasn't an object. Blake was a Fortune, and besides his family owning the largest corporation in the western part of South Dakota—maybe the entire state—he was quite a successful businessman and multimillionaire in his own right.

"I was thinking—"

He suddenly placed his finger to her lips, stopping her. "It's past five, Sasha. The business day is over and it's time for pleasure."

"But—"

She intended to tell him that business was the only reason she'd come to Deadwood. But when he wrapped his arms around her and pulled her to him, the words stuck in her suddenly dry throat and all thoughts of a promotional campaign flew right out of her head.

"You know what they say about all work and no play, Sasha."

"Th-they make a person dull?" Her mind told her to push him away, but her body refused to cooperate.

As if in slow motion, she watched him nod his head, then smiling, lower his forehead to hers. "Remember, you're not only here on business. You're here to get away for a weekend. And I'm personally going to see to it that you relax and have a little fun while you're in town."

His smoldering blue gaze held hers until she felt as if she might melt into a puddle at his feet. Then, just when she thought he was going to kiss her, the doors swished open. Releasing her, he stepped back for her to exit the elevator ahead of him.

The tendons in her knees felt loose and rubbery as she walked out into the hall, and she found it extremely difficult to draw air into her lungs. Dear heavens, he hadn't even kissed her and she was about to lose it.

Taking first one breath, then another, she wondered if her luggage had been delivered to her room. Earlier in the day, Blake had sent his driver to take her small bag to the Belle while he'd shown her around the Lucky Fortune. Hopefully, it would be waiting for her. And if she had any sense, she'd pick it up and call for someone to take her to the airfield. Or if there weren't any outgoing flights this evening, she could find a car to rent and drive back to Sioux Falls without waiting to see what he'd do next.

"Which room is supposed to be mine?" she asked, desperately hoping she didn't sound as breathless as she felt.

"This way," Blake said, moving to her side to open a door with Riverboat Queen engraved on an ornate wood-and-brass plaque.

When she walked into the suite, Sasha marveled at the beautiful antique decor. The living area had been decorated like a nineteenth-century parlor and it appeared no detail had been overlooked. From the floral-print rug on the hardwood floor to the flocked wallpaper and wainscoting on the walls, it was meant to make the occupant feel as if they'd taken a step back in time and had boarded a real riverboat.

"Are all the rooms decorated like this?" she asked, letting curiosity get the better of her.

"No. Only the suites." He opened the door to the

bedroom. "Standard accommodations are pretty much like any other hotel room."

When she walked into the bedroom, her breath caught at the sight of the huge poster bed with a lace canopy and matching crocheted bedspread. "This is absolutely gorgeous, Blake."

A half smile curved the corners of his mouth and she could tell her comment pleased him. "When I bought the Belle some people thought I was crazy to insist the decorator use real antiques for the high-end suites. But it's been a big hit with those looking for the old West experience."

"I can understand why your guests like it," she said, spying her small suitcase. Walking over to it, she picked it up and started back across the room toward the door. "It goes along with the casino's riverboat theme and is quite charming."

His expression turned to a deep frown as he pointed to her overnight bag. "Is something wrong? Would you rather have a different suite?"

"No, this is very nice," she said, shaking her head. "But I think… That is, I…"

Her voice trailed off as she tried to think of something to say that wouldn't reveal the real reason behind her early departure. There was no way she was going to admit that the chemistry between them was about to send her into sensual shock. Opting for silence, she simply continued to stare at him.

A confident expression slowly replaced his dark scowl. "I make you nervous, don't I, Sasha?"

"D-don't be ridiculous," she stammered, wondering what had happened to the articulate, intelligent woman she'd always prided herself in being.

As he moved closer, she had to force herself not to take a step back. It would have only proven his theory right and that was something she was determined not to do.

"You want to know what I think, honey?" he asked, moving even closer.

"Not really." She did take a step back when he continued to slowly, deliberately close the distance between them.

"I think you're feeling it, the same as I am." He smiled knowingly. "And I think you want to run from it, from me."

"I don't have a clue what you're referring to, Blake."

His confident grin sent a knot to the pit of her stomach. "Liar."

She set her case down and took a step back, then another. "I don't know what you think I'm supposed to be feeling, but—"

"Don't play dumb, Sasha. It doesn't become

you." He shook his head. "We both know you're a hell of a lot smarter than that."

"All right, I'll give you that much." She felt her knees come into contact with the edge of the bed. Great. Her retreat had been stopped and he was still advancing. "But you have one thing wrong."

"What would that be?"

"I never run from anything."

At least, that was normally the case. But in this instance she wasn't certain that standing her ground would be all that smart. Especially when Creed's warning kept echoing in her ears—Blake wasn't one to be trusted.

"Really? You aren't nervous about the way I make you feel?"

Unable to make her vocal cords work, she shook her head.

He came to stand in front of her and as close as he was, if she drew in a breath—which wasn't possible at that moment—her breasts would brush the front of his sports jacket. "If that's true, Sasha, then why do you want to go back to Sioux Falls this evening? Why not stay and enjoy your weekend here?" His voice dropped when he added, "With me."

She swallowed hard as she tried to think of something to say that wouldn't refute her adamant denial. "I didn't say I was going back tonight."

"Then why did you pick up your suitcase and head for the door?" Before she could come up with a plausible excuse, he reached up to lightly chafe her lower lip with the pad of his thumb. "You aren't wanting to get back to see someone, are you?"

His light touch sent a tingling awareness skipping over every nerve in her body and she had to concentrate hard on what he'd just said. "N-no…I mean yes. That's it. There's someone I'd like to see."

His deep chuckle let her know he wasn't buying her excuse for a minute, but to her relief, he stepped away from her. "Did anyone ever tell you that you can't lie worth a damn, sweetheart?"

Drawing in some much needed air, she trembled all over as anger streaked through her. "If you'll remember, I'm here at your request for help with your promotion. Nothing more."

As they stared at each other like two prize fighters sizing up their opponent, the phone on the bedside table rang several times before she finally reached over to answer it. She had no idea who the caller could be, but whomever it was, she definitely owed them a debt of gratitude.

"H-hello?"

"Sasha, are you all right?" Creed's deep voice was a welcome sound.

"Hi, Creed. I'm fine. Why do you ask?" At the mention of his brother's name, she watched Blake's easy smile disappear and his eyes narrow dangerously.

"You sounded a little shook up when you answered the phone." She heard him release a frustrated breath. "You know I don't trust that son of a bitch. I guess I was reading something more into the tone of your voice than was there."

"I suppose so," she said, careful to keep her voice as noncommittal as possible. From the dark frown on Blake's handsome face, he wasn't happy to hear that his brother was on the other end of the line, nor did he intend to leave the room until she'd ended the phone call. "Was there something you needed, Creed?"

"Not really." From the slight hesitancy in his voice, she could imagine his sheepish grin. "I was a little worried about you and I wanted to make sure you're being treated well."

"I am."

"Good," he said, sounding a little more at ease. "Just remember, if you have any problems all you have to do is give me a call. I'll be more than happy to fly down to Deadwood and give that jerk an attitude adjustment."

"Thank you, that means a lot, Creed." She

couldn't help but smile at her friend's concern. "I'll see you Monday morning."

When she hung up the phone, Blake's expression was congenial enough, but there was a spark of anger in the depths of his blue gaze that sent a chill coursing through her. "Your boyfriend checking up on you?"

"Creed and I are good friends, but that's as far as it goes," she said, wondering why she felt the need to explain her relationship with his brother.

He stared at her for several more seconds before he spoke again. "I have a couple of things I need to take care of," he finally said. "Change into something more casual and I'll come back in about an hour to take you to dinner."

"Is that an order, Mr. Fortune?" Her irritation with his high-handedness returned tenfold.

His expression became unreadable a moment before he shook his head and pointed to her black suit. "I just figured you'd want to trade your skirt and heels for something more comfortable."

"There's no need for you to come back up here. I'll meet you downstairs in the restaurant," she said when he turned to leave.

He looked as if he intended to say something. Instead, he gave her a short nod and without another word left the room.

When Sasha heard the outer door close, she

finally released the breath she was certain she'd been holding from the moment they'd entered the suite. What on earth had she done? More importantly, why had she let Blake get to her?

She'd had every intention of leaving when they'd walked into the suite. And if she hadn't let his goading rile her, she'd be on her way to the airfield at that very moment.

But no. She couldn't leave well enough alone. He'd been so sure of himself, she'd taken up the challenge and had been determined to prove him wrong. Unfortunately, the only thing she'd accomplished was doing what he wanted her to do in the first place—to spend the weekend with him in Deadwood.

Shaking her head, she couldn't help but wonder what she'd gotten herself into. Or, more importantly, how she was going to get out of it.

The second Sasha stepped off the elevator and walked toward the entrance of the Golden Belle Restaurant, Blake watched several men in the lobby turn to stare at the auburn-haired beauty in the jade silk pantsuit. Her slender body moved with a sensual grace that he found absolutely fascinating and he took a moment to enjoy the view.

Blake was going to enjoy sharing a physical relationship with Sasha. The chemistry between them was utterly amazing. He couldn't keep his hands off her. And her reaction to his touch, her breathlessness whenever he came near her, indicated that she found him to be every bit as compelling.

But he'd have to be careful not to put too much pressure on her, too soon. He'd have to take his time and romance her in order to prove that whatever Creed had told her about him had been erroneous.

Gritting his teeth at the thought of Creed's interrupting phone call, Blake had to force himself to calm down. He'd thought that by acting like Creed, it would win her over. But it was clear she was tired of the bulldozer approach to romance.

All Blake had to do was change tactics, turn on the charm and Sasha would be his for the taking. He could be himself and old Creed would take care of the rest. Knowing his half brother the way he did, Blake was confident that Creed would keep reminding her of his suspicions, continue to make phone calls to check up on her and ultimately push her right into Blake's waiting arms.

He smiled as he watched Sasha standing by the entrance to the restaurant, obviously waiting for him. She was a captivating woman and he wasn't the only one who thought so. Apparently, the men who had turned to watch her walk across the lobby found her just as mesmerizing. One in particular caught Blake's attention when the man approached Sasha to strike up a conversation.

For reasons he didn't care to analyze, a wave of possessiveness shot through Blake and he wasted no time in moving in to stake his claim. "You're late, sweetheart." He met the interloper's curious gaze with a cold smile as he slipped his arm around Sasha's shoulders. "You'll have to excuse us. We're on our way to dinner." He nodded toward the casino. "And I'm sure you'd like to get back to the action."

The man returned Blake's stare for several silent seconds, then lifting the drink he held, he nodded a silent concession. "Have a nice dinner."

As the man descended the steps into the casino area, Sasha turned on Blake. "Are you always that rude to your guests?"

Sliding his hand down her back to cup her elbow, he steered her back toward the elevators. "Are you in the habit of encouraging men to hit on you?"

"Not that it's any of your business, but all he wanted from me was to see if I knew what time it was," she said, clearly exasperated.

Blake grunted. "Yeah, and I'm Buffalo Bill Cody."

When the elevator doors opened, she stopped dead in her tracks. "Why are we going back upstairs? I thought we were going to dinner."

"We are." He urged her forward, then pushed the button for the top floor. "I had the staff set up our dinner in my suite."

"Why?" If her expression was any indication, she was anything but happy about the arrangement and more than a little suspicious of his motives.

"I thought it would give us a chance to talk un-interrupted and catch up on old times," he said, shrugging.

She looked at him as if she thought he might be a few cards shy of a full deck. "Catch up on old times? Since I started working at Dakota Fortune, we've only spoken briefly at the office and a few times at the social functions I've attended with Creed."

His gut burned at the mention of his half brother's name, but Blake stifled the urge to curse aloud. The success of his mission depended on him keeping a cool head.

When the elevators doors opened, he guided her down the hall toward his suite. "You're forgetting that we attended the same high school."

She shook her head. "Don't feed me that line, Blake Fortune. You didn't have the slightest notion that I existed back then."

"That's where you're wrong, Sasha." Opening the door to the Admiral's Suite, Blake stood back for her to enter his private domain. "I would have had to be as blind as a damned bat not to have noticed one of the prettiest girls in school." He smiled. "And I've never had vision problems."

"Give me a break." She rolled her eyes. "We had a photography class together for one semester and in that whole time, I don't remember a single instance of you speaking to me."

Walking up to stand in front of her, he touched her soft cheek with his index finger. "Believe me, sweetheart, I found out all I could about you after that first day of class. But you were too young for me back then."

"There's only…three years difference in our ages." To his satisfaction, she sounded a little breathless and confirmed his suspicions beyond a shadow of doubt that she was still attracted to him.

Smiling, he shook his head. "I was a typical eighteen-year-old boy with a raging case of hormones. I wanted a whole lot more from a girl than sharing a few chaste kisses. And let's face it, Sasha, at fifteen that's all you were ready for."

"Why are you telling me this now, Blake?" Her confusion was reflected in her luminous green eyes and he didn't think he'd ever seen her look more desirable.

He was going to enjoy his seduction of Sasha

Kilgore. But it was time to back off a little and let her catch up.

Deciding it would be in his best interest to put a little space between them, he guided her over to the table his staff had set up by the window overlooking Deadwood's historic district below. "I told you. We're talking about old times, sweetheart." He held her chair, then seated himself on the opposite side of the small round table. "You were in the chorus weren't you?"

"Yes, but you weren't."

The flicker of the small candle on the table between them brought out the highlights of golden red in her auburn hair, fascinating him. "That doesn't mean I don't remember your singing at my graduation."

"Oh, dear," she said, her cheeks coloring a pretty pink. "You remember that?"

"It was quite an honor for a freshman to be asked to sing a solo at another class's graduation," he said, nodding.

He'd anticipated her wanting to know what he remembered about her and he'd done his homework in advance. Besides thumbing through his high-school annual, Blake had spent several hours trying to think of all the times their paths had crossed during his last year of school.

The color on her cheeks deepened. "Having to perform in front of all those people made me a nervous wreck. That's when I decided to limit my singing to the shower."

"That's a shame. You have a beautiful voice and did a wonderful job with the song." Reaching across the table, he took her hand in his. "I'd like to hear you sing again sometime, sweetheart." He smiled and before he could stop himself, he added, "My shower has great acoustics."

Her eyes widened a moment before anger filled their green depths. "I don't think so."

"Never say never, Sasha."

She pulled her hand from his and, pushing her chair back, rose to her feet. "I don't know what you're up to, Blake Fortune. But it's not going to work."

Rising to face her, he didn't think twice about taking her into his arms and drawing her to him. "I'm not up to anything more than having dinner with a beautiful woman that for years, I've wanted to get to know better."

He heard the hitch in her breath a moment before she trembled against him. "Why now? Why after all these years are you—"

"Hush, Sasha."

Before she had the chance to question him

further, Blake lowered his mouth to hers and at the first contact, he felt as if he'd been hit by a bolt of lightning. Nothing could have prepared him for his reaction to the softness of her perfect lips, yielding to the demands of his.

But it was her response that had him hard in less than two seconds flat and forgetting all about slowing things down. Resistant at first, when she melted against him, her fingers curled into the front of his shirt as if she needed to hold on to him to keep from falling at his feet.

As he tightened his arms around her and continued kissing her, a tiny moan escaped her slightly parted lips and he took advantage of her acquiescence to slip his tongue inside. Blake acquainted himself with her tender inner recesses, exploring her thoroughly, savoring the sweetness that was uniquely Sasha.

He slid his hands from her back, up along her sides to the underside of her breasts, but stopped just short of cupping the soft mounds. He sensed that too much, too soon would only scare her away. And that was the last thing he wanted to do.

Reluctant to completely break contact with her, he held her slender body close as he eased away from the kiss. Neither spoke, but he could tell that he'd accomplished two of his goals. He'd managed to stop her from arguing with him, as well as establishing the direction he intended for their friendship to go.

Three

As Sasha sat, staring at Blake across the elegantly arranged table, she had no idea what she was eating or how it tasted. After that kiss, she was lucky to remember her own name, let alone take notice of the food on her plate.

When she'd been a teenager, she'd fantasized about him holding her, kissing her. But she'd never thought the dream would come true. Nor could she have imagined eleven years ago how his kiss would affect her. It had been at least fifteen minutes since they'd sat back down for dinner and she still felt as if every cell in her body tingled.

"How is your steak?" he asked, pointing to her plate.

She stared at the filet mignon, amazed that she'd eaten almost half of it without recalling a single bite. "Uh…very good."

His pleased smile caused a little flutter deep down in the most secret part of her. "I had the new chef I hired for Fortune's Gold prepare the meal for us. I intend to include an intimate dinner for two as part of the high-end package I'll be offering and wanted your opinion on ways to improve it."

Glancing at the table, Sasha shook her head. "I can't think of anything to improve on this. The food is delicious and the use of fine china, instead of the heavier restaurant plates, is a wonderful idea. I also think the sterling-silver candle holders add an elegant touch. I'm sure this will be quite popular with honeymooning couples."

"Or lovers wanting a romantic weekend getaway," he said, lowering his voice as he placed his hand atop hers where it rested on the pristine tablecloth.

The suggestive sound of his smooth voice and the promising look in his dark-blue eyes set her pulse racing and caused a delicious little shiver to slide up her spine. Everything she thought she'd wanted at the age of fifteen was coming true. Blake Fortune had not only noticed her, it appeared that he intended to sweep her off her feet.

But she was finding it extremely difficult to believe that the object of her adolescent dreams had finally noticed her. "What do you really want from me, Blake?" she asked as she carefully placed her fork on the edge of the delicate china plate.

"I told you, sweetheart. I need your help with the ad campaign." He gave her a smile that made her feel warm all over. "And I'm using it as an excuse to get to know you better. Something I should have done a long time ago."

He seemed sincere enough, but Creed's warning that Blake couldn't be trusted continued to whisper at the back of her mind. Had her friend been right about his brother? Could Blake be up to something underhanded?

But it made no sense. What would he possibly stand to gain? She certainly couldn't give him any information about Dakota Fortune that he didn't already have access to.

The feel of his palm gently caressing the back of her hand sent the fluttering in the pit of her stomach into overdrive and ended all speculation about his possible ulterior motives. "I…um, think I'd…uh, better go back to my room," she said, extricating her hand from his. She suddenly found it extremely hard to form a coherent thought and she needed to put some distance between them in order to regain her equilibrium. "I'm really tired and I think it's time for me to call it a night."

She could tell by the expression on his handsome face that he wasn't buying her excuse for a minute, but scooting his chair away from the table, he rose to his feet and offered her his hand. "I'll walk you back to your suite."

"Th-that won't be necessary." His much larger hand enveloping hers as she stood up made her feel as if the temperature in the room had gone up a good ten degrees. "I'm pretty sure I can find my way to the other end of the hall."

Putting his arm around her shoulders, he shook his head as they walked to the door. "If there was one thing that Nash Fortune taught his boys, it was proper date etiquette."

"D-date?"

Guiding them out into the hall, he chuckled. "Whether it's business or pleasure, when a man asks a woman he has more than a passing interest in to have dinner with him, it's a date."

She shook her head as she pulled her key card from her small evening bag. "You didn't ask me to have dinner with you. It was more of a command."

He took the card from her, fitted it into the lock, then after opening the door, stood back for her to enter the suite. "Considering you were about to take off, I didn't feel that you gave me much of a choice."

Turning to face him, she asked, "In other words, as a board member of Dakota Fortune, you were pulling rank on me?"

Shrugging one shoulder, he gave her a lopsided grin and pulled her into his arms. "I hadn't thought of it that way, but whatever works."

Sasha caught her breath at the feel of his solid strength pressed against her from her breasts to her knees. "Wh-what do you think you're doing?"

"I'm going to kiss you good-night," he said, his voice so low and hypnotic that she felt as if she'd spontaneously combust at any moment. "That's usually the way a first date ends, honey."

Before she could remind him that she didn't consider their dinner a date, he lowered his head and captured her lips with his. That was when Sasha ceased thinking altogether and gave in to the temptation of once again experiencing the power of Blake's sultry kiss.

Firm and commanding, his mouth moved over hers with a masterfulness that caused her head to spin. But when he parted her lips with his tongue to slip inside, he not only robbed her of breath, he left her with nothing but the ability to respond.

Tasting of wine and pure male desire, he explored her thoroughly as he stroked and teased. Sasha wondered if she'd ever be the same again when he slid his hands from her back along her sides and up to the swell of her breasts.

Her skin tingled when he broke the kiss to nibble his way to the sensitive hollow at the base of her throat. "Y-you're taking this…farther than a simple… good-night kiss," she said, struggling to breathe.

"Do you want me to stop?"

His warm breath and the vibration of his masculine voice against her skin had Sasha feeling as if a spark ignited within her soul. But when he covered her breasts with his hands to test their weight and tease the suddenly tightened tips through the layers of her clothing, her body began to tremble and she had to force herself to concentrate on what he'd asked her.

"N-no… Y-yes."

Why was she having such a hard time gathering her thoughts? And why couldn't she tell him outright that she wanted him to stop?

"You want to know what I think, Sasha?"

"Not…really." Drawing air into her lungs was becoming decidedly more difficult with each teasing brush of his thumbs over her taut nipples. And like it or not, she really didn't want him to stop.

Moving his hands to her back to draw her more fully against him, he nuzzled the hair at her temple. "I think you need to get a good night's sleep. If we're going to visit a couple of museums and spend some time introducing you to some of the casino games, you'll need your rest." Kissing her forehead, he released her, then walked to the door. "Good night, Sasha."

As she stood there waiting for her head to quit spinning, he turned to give her a smile warm enough to melt her bones. Then, just when she thought he was going to cross the room and take her back into his arms, he walked out into the hall and quietly pulled the door shut behind him.

Staring at the closed door for several long seconds, she finally managed to breathe normally as she slipped off her pumps and slowly made her way into the bedroom. She wasn't certain her rubbery legs would support her for the short distance, let alone allow her to balance herself on a pair of high heels.

She should have left earlier in the evening as she'd intended, she thought as she changed out of her jade silk pantsuit and into her baby-doll pajamas. She was so far out of her league with Blake, they weren't even in the same ballpark.

But as she unfastened the clip holding her hair in its tight chignon, then slipped between the crisp linen sheets on the big four-poster bed, she had to be honest with herself. Although she was completely out of her element with Blake, she'd never felt more exhilarated or alive in her entire life.

Blake pulled his cell phone from his belt as he pushed the breakfast cart down the hall toward the Riverboat Queen Suite. After walking Sasha back to her room last night, he'd spent several sleepless hours rethinking his approach for getting her into his bed and came to several conclusions.

Thanks to his brother, she was clearly wary of him and more than a little confused by his interest after all this time. That was why he'd have to pull out all the stops in romancing Sasha Kilgore. It might take a little more time than he'd anticipated, which didn't set too well. But in retrospect, it would heighten the pleasure when they finally did make love.

Dialing directly into her room, he waited for Sasha to answer.

"Hello." Her voice was slightly husky from sleep and caused an unexpected rush of heat to zing through his veins.

"Good morning, sleepyhead."

"Blake?"

"None other."

"Why are you calling me at—" He heard the rustle of bed sheets and could imagine her sitting up in bed to push her hair out of her eyes and look at the clock. "Dear God, it's only six-thirty."

He laughed. "Get out of bed and open the door to your suite, Sasha."

"Why?"

"Do you always ask this many questions?"

"Do you always answer a question with a question?" she retorted.

"Just open the damned door."

"All right, but this had better be good," she grumbled, hanging up the phone.

When she flung open the door a few moments later, Blake smiled as he pushed the cart into the room. Sasha looked about as sexy as he'd ever seen a woman. Her pretty face wore the blush of sleep and her long auburn hair tumbled well past her shoulders in a wild array of soft curls.

But it was the sight of her long slender legs that sent his blood pressure soaring. Her teal silk robe was one of those short numbers that ended about mid-thigh and revealed more than it covered.

Deciding that it would be in his best interest not

to point out that particular fact, he opted for discussing her mood. "I take it you're not a morning person."

"And I take it you are." Waving her hand toward the covered plates and silver coffee carafe, she arched one perfect eyebrow. "Please tell me that's for someone else."

"Can't do that, sweetheart," he said, taking plates from the cart to place then on the small table by the window. "I thought we would have breakfast together before we head out for the day."

She frowned as she shook her head. "I never eat this early in the morning."

But she did follow him across the room and stood there looking so damned adorable, he'd have liked nothing more than to take her into the bedroom and have her for breakfast. Instead, he wisely motioned for her to sit down.

"Experts say that breakfast is the most important meal of the day."

"Those so-called experts are no doubt morning people that the rest of us would like to string up by their toes," she groused, sinking into one of the chairs. "At least, until after we've consumed several cups of coffee."

He laughed as he poured them both a mug of the

rich, dark brew. "Please, drink up. I'd like to keep my toes safe."

To his satisfaction, she picked up the cup, held it up to appreciate the aroma, then closing her eyes, smiled. "Mmm. How did you know I love mocha-flavored coffee?"

He seated himself in the chair across from her. "I haven't met a woman yet who doesn't think that anything chocolate is almost as good as making love."

Opening her eyes, she stared at him over the rim of the cup as she took a sip of the rich brew. "Oh, really. And what do you prefer?"

He grinned. "Sex, of course."

Clearly embarrassed, she shook her head. "I meant what flavor of coffee."

"I know, but you didn't phrase it that way." Changing the subject before he said something that got him into deeper trouble with her than he was already in, he removed the covers from their plates. "I didn't know how you like your eggs. I hope scrambled is to your liking."

"That's fine, and I do appreciate your thoughtfulness, but—"

Before she could protest further, Blake picked up her fork, speared some of the fluffy eggs and put it into her mouth. "Now, isn't that good?"

She glared at him as she chewed, then swallowing, she nodded as she reached for the fork. "Yes."

He held the utensil away. "You want more?"

"Yes."

She said the word grudgingly and from the look on her face, he decided it wouldn't move them any closer to the physical relationship he wanted if he seized the opportunity to gloat. Handing her the fork, he picked up his own and for the next few minutes they ate in companionable silence.

"When do you want me to present my proposal for your ad campaign?" she asked as she poured herself another cup of coffee.

"You've already worked it up?" He didn't particularly want to discuss business. He had other, more enjoyable pursuits in mind.

To his relief, she shook her head. "I have a few more things to go over, but I should have it ready by this afternoon."

"I don't think so."

"Excuse me?"

"Today is your day off." He reached out to take her hand in his. "I promised you a day of fun and that's exactly what we're going to have." He raised her palm to his lips and kissed her tender skin. "Now, go get dressed so we can get started."

"Wh-what on earth could we possibly do at

this hour of the morning?" Her voice sounded a little shaky. "The museums won't open for several more hours."

It was all he could do to keep from telling her what he wanted to do and how he'd like to spend the day with her in bed. "Sweetheart, casinos are open 24/7."

As if she suddenly realized that he still held her hand, she extricated it from his. "I've never gambled before and wouldn't even begin to know how to play any of the games."

He smiled. "It's pretty simple and it will be my pleasure to teach you." He rose to his feet, walked over to the phone on the desk and dialed room service. While he waited for one of the staff to pick up, he motioned toward the bedroom. "Get dressed while I get someone up here to clear the table."

"Is that an order or a suggestion?"

From the look on her face, he could tell that he'd better watch the way he phrased things. "I was merely suggesting that you might want to put something on." He grinned. "I love the hell out of the way you look in that little silk robe, but you might give one of my waiters a coronary when he sees your long, sexy bare legs."

Sasha's heart raced as she glanced down at her robe. She hadn't considered its length when she'd packed yesterday morning and the only male that had ever seen her in it was Melvin. Of course, besides being a big yellow cat, Melvin had been neutered several years ago and couldn't care less about females, feline or human.

But Blake was an entirely different matter. He was a virile, twenty-nine-year-old man who exuded sexual charm from every pore of his skin. Unfortunately, she'd been so irritated by being awakened at what she considered to be an ungodly hour, she hadn't given the length of her robe a second thought. But from the look on his face, he'd definitely been thinking about it. A lot.

Giving the hem a little tug in a futile effort to make it longer, she edged her way to the bedroom door. "I think I'll…uh, go change."

Her heart-rate accelerated even more when Blake winked and gave her a wicked smile. "Good idea. And make sure it's something casual and comfortable."

Nodding, she slipped into the bedroom and closing the doors, made a beeline for her suitcase. As she gathered her things for a quick shower, she tried not to put much stock in Blake's flirting. She had a feeling the man wasn't above using whatever means it took to get what he wanted. The only problem was she had no idea what Blake could possibly want from her beyond her proposal for the ad campaign.

Could it really be as he'd said? Did he really just want to get to know her better?

As she toweled herself off and dressed, she came to the conclusion that Creed's warnings about Blake had stemmed from the hard feelings between the two brothers and weren't really a reflection of Blake's character. From everything she'd seen, Blake was just as he appeared—a highly successful businessman who not only wanted her to design a promotional campaign for his casinos, he was interested in getting to know her on a more personal level.

"The man you've dreamed about half of your life has finally discovered that you exist and you're having second thoughts about becoming involved with him?" she asked herself as she twisted her unruly hair into a tight knot at the back of her head. "Are you insane?"

But as she put on her mascara, gathered her jacket and prepared to join Blake in the suite's living room, she decided that her mind wasn't what worried her. If she let herself go and gave in to his charismatic charm, it was her heart that could very well be in danger of being lost.

"Blake, this is ridiculous," Sasha laughed when he motioned for her to push a stack of poker chips into the middle of a circle on the green felted table.

After touring the town's museums chronicling Deadwood's colorful history and having a scrumptious lunch at Blake's other hotel and casino, the Lucky Fortune, they had returned to the Belle of Fortune for her to try her hand at a few games of chance. Blake had a man he'd called the pit boss set up a private table for him to teach her the various card games and she was finding that although they were fun, she'd starve to death if she had to make a living in the world of professional gambling.

Blake leaned close when the dealer shuffled, then dealt the cards. "The dealer is showing a six and has to stay on seventeen," Blake whispered closely to her ear. "You have twelve and the odds are in your favor to win the hand. Take another card."

The feel of his warm breath on her overly sensitive skin distracted her from the game. Taking a deep breath, she used every ounce of willpower she had to react normally. "Are you sure? What if the card the dealer has facing down is an ace? Then he'd have eighteen and there's the possibility I'd lose."

Blake nodded. "That's true. But that's why it's called gambling. You have to take the chance in order to come out ahead."

"But—"

He softly touched her chin with his index finger and turned her head until their gazes met. "Sweetheart, life is full of risks. Sometimes you win. Sometimes you lose. But keep in mind, there's a fifty-fifty chance that the risks you don't take could have been missed opportunities."

Her heart skipped several beats as she gazed into his amazing blue eyes. There was a challenge there and she knew beyond a shadow doubt, he was talking about her taking a chance on a whole lot more than just a hand of cards.

"I don't know," she said uncertainly.

She wasn't sure she had the courage to risk becoming involved with Blake. She could very well end up with a broken heart, as well as having her pride completely shattered.

"Take a break," he said to the dealer, standing patiently awaiting her decision on the hand of cards. As the man silently nodded and walked away, Blake turned her to face him. "Give me a chance, Sasha. Give *us* a chance."

She shook her head. "There is no *us*."

"Not yet." His smile sent a wave of heat from the top of her head all the way to her toes. "But I intend for there to be."

Her heart stopped completely at the determination in his voice and the promise in his eyes. He'd abandoned his earlier excuse of wanting to get to know her better and moved straight to them becoming romantically involved.

The thrill of anticipation skipped up her spine as his gaze held her captive and he slowly lowered his head to brush his lips against hers. But when he settled his mouth over hers in a kiss so tender it robbed her of all rational thought, she forgot all the reasons that taking a chance on caring for Blake could prove her undoing—or that they were sitting in the middle of a crowded casino. Nothing seemed to matter but the sudden heat coursing through her and the need to lean into his embrace. Without a second thought, she raised her arms to circle his neck and tangle her fingers in the silky hair at his nape.

When she pressed herself to his chest, his arms closed around her and he slipped his tongue inside to deepen the kiss. Colorful lights immediately began to flash behind Sasha's closed eyes and it felt as if the world had been reduced to just the two of them when he slowly stroked her inner recesses and coaxed her into responding in kind. But when he effortlessly lifted her from her chair to sit her on his lap, a delicious tingling sensation began to flow throughout her body and a tiny moan escaped her parted lips at the feel of his rapidly hardening body through the layers of their clothing.

"Way to go, man." The sudden sound of a laughing male voice made Sasha's heart stop.

When she tried to jerk from his arms, Blake held her firmly against him as he eased his lips from hers and slowly turned his head to glare at a young man standing a few feet from their table. Blake didn't say a word. He didn't have to. His menacing look was enough to wipe the leering expression from the man's face and had him disappearing into the crowd without so much as a moment's hesitation.

Sasha's cheeks felt as if they were on fire and she couldn't have found her voice if her life depended on it. What on earth had gotten into her? She'd never in her entire life been the type to get so caught up in a kiss that she forgot where she was. Nor had she ever been one for public displays of affection.

Dear heavens, what would have happened if the kiss had been more passionate or lasted longer? Mortified, she buried her face against Blake's broad shoulder. There was no doubt in her mind that she would have made an even bigger fool of herself than she already had.

As if sensing that she would rather be anywhere else than in the middle of a crowded casino, Blake set her on her feet and stood up beside her. "That's enough of the blackjack lessons for one day. It's dinnertime anyway and I'm sure our table is ready."

Before she could find her voice and tell him that what she really needed was to be alone, he took her by the hand and walked toward the Golden Belle. Once they were seated at a small table in a cozy little corner at the back of the restaurant, he reached up to stroke her cheek with his index finger.

"Sasha, I'm not going to mince words." His promising smile sent a wave of excitement coursing through her. "I want you and I'm not going to stop until I make you mine."

Four

Thanking the powers that be for a few moments to herself, Sasha sat in the Golden Belle and thoughtfully sipped her coffee as she waited for Blake to return. He'd been called away on casino business right after they'd finished dinner and it was the first opportunity she'd had to contemplate his bold statement about making her his.

What on earth was she going to do? Did she have the courage to become involved with him?

All of her adult life she'd used extreme caution when it came to relationships. She'd witnessed some of her friends and coworkers suffer through the misery of failure and she'd been determined not to find herself in the same position.

Unfortunately, she wasn't entirely certain she had a choice where Blake was concerned. From the moment she'd laid eyes on him in high school, she'd been attracted to him. And although she'd convinced herself she'd gotten over her schoolgirl crush years ago, she was finding him even more irresistible now than she had eleven years ago.

She sighed heavily as the object of her affection walked into the restaurant, spoke to the hostess, then walked toward her. If Creed was right about Blake, she could very well end up emotionally shattered. But how in the world could she make herself immune to his charms?

"I'm sorry about a being called away," he said, smiling apologetically as he pulled out the chair across from her and sat down. "There was a minor altercation at one of the craps tables and they needed me in the security office to smooth over the situation with one of our whales."

"I hope it wasn't serious."

He shook his head. "The man had a little too much to drink and accused another guest of stealing part of his chip stack."

"Was the guest in question guilty?"

"No." Blake grinned. "The whale's wife had

taken them and cashed them in to keep her husband from losing more than he already had."

Sasha laughed. "I can understand her caution. The thought of losing a lot of money on something as frivolous as a game would drive me insane." Wondering if there was ever any real danger of fights breaking out, she asked, "Do things like a disagreement between two guests ever come to blows?"

"No. My security team is one of the best in Deadwood and they're on top of a situation like this before it ever comes to that." He reached across the table to take her hand in his. "But I don't want to talk about that now."

A warmth began to flow through her from the feel of his hand caressing hers. "W-would you like to discuss my ideas for your promotional campaign?" she hedged, hoping to buy a little more time to sort out what she was going to do.

"No, sweetheart. The last thing I want to do is talk business with you." Lifting her hand to his lips, he kissed the rapidly beating pulse at the base of her wrist. "We'll go over your suggestions tomorrow." He gave her a meaningful look. "I intend for tonight to be all about us."

Sasha swallowed hard. "I haven't exactly agreed to there being an *us*."

His smile caused her whole body to tingle. "Yes, you have."

"I—I don't recall...that happening. W-would you...care to refresh...my memory?" she asked, suddenly finding it hard to make her voice work.

"Your response when I kissed you this afternoon in the casino was all the answer I needed."

His lips grazing the sensitive skin along her wrist caused her to shiver. "I—"

"Don't try to deny it, sweetheart. You're as attracted to me as I am to you." His voice dropped seductively. "You're trembling now from just talking about it."

Sasha couldn't think of a thing to say. What could she say? He was right and they both knew it.

"Come on," he said, rising to his feet and pulling her up to stand beside him. "Let's go upstairs to my suite."

Her heart fluttered erratically. "I'm not sure... that's a good idea."

His low chuckle sent a wave of heat streaking straight to her inner core. "I think it's an excellent idea." He placed his hand to the small of her back and leaning close, added, "Before the evening is over with, I'm going to make sure you do, too."

Try as she might, Sasha couldn't stop the feeling of nervous anticipation building inside of her. No

matter what Creed said about Blake being untrust-
worthy, no matter how foolish it might turn out to
be or how high a price she could very well end up
paying, she was going to follow her heart and see
where it led her with Blake.

She sighed as they left the restaurant. If she was
perfectly honest with herself, she'd have to admit
that she'd never had a choice in the matter.

When they entered his suite, Blake's mouth went
completely dry as he noticed the seductive sway of
Sasha's hips while she walked over to stare out the
window at the street below. The clingy black dress
she wore hugged her like a lover's caress and she
was without a doubt the sexiest woman he'd ever
had the privilege to lay eyes on.

Blake smiled coldly. His brother had been a
damned fool to let her make the trip to Deadwood
alone and it was going to serve Creed right to lose
her. The bastard didn't deserve a woman as special
as Sasha and before the night was over, Blake was
going to convince her of that fact.

But the thought of his brother holding Sasha,
touching her flawless skin and losing himself in her
soft body caused a burning deep in the pit of
Blake's belly and a sudden, uncontrollable need to

stake his claim. Tonight he was going to take her into his arms and make her his.

Walking up behind her, he wrapped his arms around her waist and drew her back against him. "Do you have any idea how beautiful you are?"

She shook her head. "I have too many flaws. My hair is—"

"Gorgeous," he interrupted, nuzzling the side of her slender neck.

"I—I've never liked…my hair," she said, sounding extremely short of breath. "It's always been too hard…to tame."

"You used to wear it down when we were in school," he said, reaching up to release the pins she used to hold it in place. Free of their confinement, the silky curls cascaded over his hands like a cinnamon-colored waterfall. "Your hair is soft and feminine." He turned her to face him and, lowering his head, added, "And it compliments your creamy skin to perfection."

As he fused their lips, Blake slid his hands from her shoulders to her hips and pulled her closer. The feel of her soft body pressed closely to his, the smell of her herbal-scented hair and her sweet taste as she melted against him quickly had him hard with need.

Allowing her to feel his rapidly changing body, he caught her to him and when a tiny moan escaped her slightly parted lips, he seized the opportunity to slip his tongue inside. He explored her with a thoroughness that left them both aching for more. Encouraged by her response, he continued to stroke her tender inner recesses as he slid his hands up to the underside of her breasts.

She stiffened for a split second as if she intended to protest when he used his thumbs to tease the tightened tips through the stretchy black fabric of her dress. Then to his satisfaction, she reached up to put her arms around his neck and leaned into his touch. She might have been resistant to him when she'd first arrived in Deadwood, but her body was telling him all he needed to know about her receptiveness to his advances now.

"So sweet," he said, breaking the kiss to nibble his way down the column of her slender neck. "So damned sexy."

"I—I should go back…to my room," she said haltingly.

"Is that what you really want, sweetheart?"

"N-no. I mean yes." She closed her eyes and took a deep breath. "I can't…think clearly."

He chuckled as he kissed the fluttering pulse at the base of her throat. "Would you like to hear what I think?"

"N-not really."

Leaning back, he gazed into her pretty green

eyes. "I think you need to stay right here with me tonight. In my suite. In my bed. In my arms."

"I can't…do that." Her tone was breathy and not at all convincing.

"Yes, you can." He brushed his lips over hers. "You want me as much as I want you."

She opened her eyes and, staring at him, slowly shook her head. "I—"

"Don't try to deny it, Sasha." He grazed his thumbs over her taut nipples as he pressed himself against her and smiled at the shiver he felt course through her when she felt the hard ridge of his arousal. "Your body is telling me everything I need to know."

"W-we shouldn't."

"Why not?" He nipped at her collarbone. "We're not kids anymore. We're both consenting adults with a desire to find pleasure with each other."

She closed her eyes as she tilted her head back to give him better access. "I've never—"

"This won't be a one-night stand," he interrupted, anticipating what she was about to tell him.

"But that's not—"

"Are you committed to Creed?"

She frowned as she shook her head. "I told you, your brother and I are nothing more than just good friends."

He still had a hard time believing that Creed had spent the last year with Sasha and not taken their friendship to a more personal level. "If that's the case, then there's no reason for you to go back to your room."

Before she could come up with any more excuses why their spending the night together was a bad idea, Blake took her back into his arms and mingled their lips in a kiss that sent a fire racing through his veins at the speed of light. When she sagged against him, he didn't think twice about swinging her up into his arms to carry her into his bedroom.

Cradled against him, her slight frame felt almost fragile and a tenderness he hadn't expected filled his chest. A woman as sweet and sexy as Sasha was meant to be loved slowly, thoroughly, and he had every intention of spending the entire night cherishing her as he was sure his brother never had.

Setting her on her feet at the side of his bed, Blake turned on the bedside lamp, then facing her, gently traced his index finger along her delicate jaw. "I'm going to spend the entire night showing you just how special you are, Sasha."

"Blake, there's something you should know," she said, looking a bit apprehensive.

"Do you want me, Sasha?"

"I shouldn't."

"That wasn't the question," he said, shaking his head. "Do you want me?"

She worried her lower lip with even white teeth a moment before she slowly nodded.

"That's all the answer I need," he said, pulling her to him.

He kissed her forehead, her eyes and the tip of her nose before lowering his mouth to hers. Her lips were sweeter than anything he'd ever tasted and he knew beyond a shadow of doubt that if he wasn't extremely careful, he could become addicted to kissing her.

As his mouth moved over hers, Sasha fleetingly wondered if she was about to make the biggest mistake of her life. But Blake was quickly robbing her of the ability to think of all the reasons making love with him could spell disaster for her and leaving her with nothing but the ability to feel.

"I'm going to love every inch of you, sweetheart," he said as he rained tiny kisses to the sensitive hollow below her ear.

A delicious tingling filled every fiber of her being and her heart began to pound erratically as he slid his hands down her back. Slowly, deliberately, he began to gather the stretchy fabric of her dress in his fists until he reached the hem.

"As sexy as you look in this little number, you're going to look even better out of it," he whispered close to her ear. "Raise your arms for me, Sasha."

Feeling as if she were in some sort of sensuous trance, she did as he commanded and in seconds she was standing before him in nothing but her underwear and a pair of black spike heels. If she'd had the chance, she might have tried covering herself, but Blake took her hands in his and held them out to her sides as his gaze caressed her from head to toe.

His sharp intake of breath, and the spark of need she detected in his dark blue eyes, made her feel more feminine and desirable than she'd ever felt in her life. "Do you always wear a garter belt…and hose?" he asked huskily.

She nodded. "I hate having to wiggle myself into a pair of panty hose."

"I'm glad," he said, grinning. "There's nothing sexier than a woman dressed in scraps of black lace and silk." He glanced down at her feet and his deep chuckle warmed her all the way to her soul. "Unless the woman is wearing a pair of high heels." When he raised his head to look at her, he gave her a smile that sent her pulse racing and caused a delightful fluttering deep in the pit of her stomach. "You're absolutely gorgeous, sweetheart."

Her cheeks heated with a mixture of embarrassment and desire. "At the moment, I'm feeling a little underdressed."

"I fully intend to remedy that," he said, shrugging out of his sports jacket. He tossed the coat onto a chair, then bent to remove his shoes and socks.

When he straightened and reached for the buttons on his shirt, Sasha tried not to stare as he released first one button, then another. But as he slid the oxford cloth from his wide shoulders, the sight of his perfectly sculpted chest, rippling stomach and lean flanks caused her to catch her breath. She'd known he kept himself in good physical condition, but she'd never dreamed that his clothes were concealing a body that could rival that of a Greek god.

As he unbuckled his belt and lowered the zipper at his fly, Sasha abandoned all pretense of nonchalance and simply stared as he slid his trousers down his muscular thighs and revealed the true magnificence of his hard body. Taut and lean, Blake Fortune was perfect in every way.

She swallowed hard when she noticed the straining outline of his erection through his white cotton briefs. He was also unquestionably aroused. The thought that she was the object of his desire caused an interesting and not at all unpleasant tightening in the most feminine part of her.

Unsure of what to do, she started to slip out of her heels, but he shook his head. "Don't. I want the pleasure of taking those off of you." He pointed to her garter belt, bra and panties. "And I'm looking forward to peeling away those little scraps of silk and lace as well."

She shivered with anticipation as she placed her hands on his wide shoulders to brace herself when he bent to remove her heels, then trailed his hands up her legs to the fastenings holding her stockings in place. As he slid the sheer nylon down her calves, Sasha caught her breath at the feel as his palms gently caressing her skin. She'd never in her entire life experienced anything quite so sensual or exciting as having Blake take off her under things, and by the time he removed her lace garter belt and satin panties, Sasha trembled uncontrollably.

He reached for her then, and holding her captive with his heated gaze, unfastened the front clasp of her bra and slowly slid it from her shoulders. "You're absolutely gorgeous," he said as he cupped her bare breasts in his large hands.

Her knees threatened to give way when he lowered his head and kissed first one tight nipple, then the other. But when he took one of the puckered buds into his mouth to tease it with his teeth and tongue, she had to brace her hands on his shoulders to keep her knees from buckling.

"You taste like peaches and cream, sweetheart."

His warm breath feathering over the moistened tip of her breast made it all but impossible to catch her breath. "If you keep that up…I'm not sure… how much longer…my legs are going to support me."

Raising his head, his smile held such promise goose bumps prickled her skin. "Let's lie down."

Before she could move to sit on the side of the bed, he reached down to pull the comforter back, then picked her up and gently placed her in the center of the wide mattress.

"I could have gotten into bed on my own, Blake."

He looked at her tenderly as he stood up and hooked his thumbs in the waistband of his briefs to pull them down. "I like the way you feel in my arms."

She would have told him that she liked having him hold her, but the words died in her throat as he slipped off his underwear and tossed them on the chair with the rest of his clothes. When he turned back toward her, Sasha's heart stalled at the sight of his impressive arousal. Although she'd seen the nude male physique, nothing could have prepared her for the reality of Blake Fortune standing before her fully aroused and looking is if he intended to devour her.

Feeling more than a little intimidated by his size and the strength of his need, she raised her eyes to meet his questioning gaze. "There's something…you probably need…to know."

He shook his head as he tucked a small foil packet beneath his pillow, then lay down beside her to gather her to him. "All I need to know is that you want me as much as I want you." He raised up on one elbow, and leaning over her, kissed his way down the slope of her breast as he skimmed his palm along her side to the swell of her hip. "You do want me to make love with you, don't you, Sasha?"

As she gazed up at him, she knew in her heart that she'd waited for this moment her entire life. She'd had other opportunities to make love with the men she'd dated, but she'd never before been able to share herself. And with crystal clarity, she suddenly realized why. None of them had been Blake Fortune.

"Yes, I want you to make love to me, Blake," she said, surprised at how steady her voice sounded, considering the amount of nervous excitement coursing through her.

He must have detected her lingering apprehension because he gave her a kiss so tender it brought tears to her eyes, then he raised his head and gave her a look that touched her heart. "I don't want you to worry, sweetheart. I promise, I'll never do anything to hurt you in any way."

Before she could tell him that she knew there would be discomfort that neither of them could avoid, he covered her lips with his and she forgot anything she was about to say. Nothing seemed to matter but the feel of his body pressed to hers and the taste of desire in his seductive kiss.

Threading her fingers through the hair at the nape of his neck, she held him to her as his tongue traced her mouth, then dipped inside to stroke, tease and coax. Shivers of delight skipped through her when he withdrew and allowed her to enter his mouth to do a little exploring of her own. She wasn't exactly sure of what she was doing, but rewarded by his groan of pleasure and the feel of his hard erection against her thigh, she decided that Blake didn't mind. Just knowing that she aroused such need in him heightened her own desire in ways she could have never imagined.

When he slowly moved his hand from her hip, down along her thigh, then up to the soft curls hiding her feminine secrets, she went perfectly still.

But the intense impulses that his touch created when he stroked her with gentle care sent a tightening heat straight to her inner core and she couldn't have stopped her moan of pleasure from escaping if her life depended on it.

Finding it all but impossible to lie still, she gripped the sheet with her fists and moved restlessly beneath his hand. "P-please—"

"Do you want me, sweetheart?"

"Y-yes." Waves of heat flowed through her as he continued to heighten her passion, but when he took her nipple into his mouth as his finger stroked her deeply, she felt as if the blood in her veins turned to liquid fire.

"Is this where you need me?" he whispered against her puckered flesh.

Unable to form a coherent thought, much less get any words out, she used her hands to raise his head from her breast and, meeting his questioning gaze, simply nodded.

Smiling, he softly kissed her lips. "That's exactly where I need to be."

As she watched, he reached beneath the pillow, removed the small foil packet and arranged their protection. Then, taking her back into his arms, he used his knee to nudge her legs apart.

When he rose above her and she felt the blunt

tip of him against her moist apex, she closed her eyes and braced herself for what would happen next. Hopefully, the discomfort would be minimal and wouldn't last too long.

"Look at me, Sasha." When she did as he commanded, the blazing passion in his dark blue eyes shook her all the way to her soul. "I don't want there to be any doubt who's making love to you."

Confused by the odd statement and the insistence in his deep voice, she started to tell him she knew exactly who she was giving her virginity to. But her voice abandoned her when he pressed his lower body forward and began to fuse their bodies into one.

"So tight," he said through clenched teeth as he continued to ease into her. But when he met the slight resistance, his eyes widened and he went completely still. "Holy hell. You're a virgin."

Five

Blake didn't move a muscle as he tried to wrap his mind around the fact that Sasha had been telling the truth. She'd never been with Creed, or for that matter, any other man.

"You're a virgin," he repeated, still unable to believe he was the first man to sink himself into her soft body.

"Was," she said, wincing as her tight body resisted the invasion of his. "I don't think that's the case anymore."

"You should have told me."

Moisture filled her pretty green eyes and he

wasn't sure if it was from the physical pain he'd caused her or the harsh accusation in the tone of his voice. Either way, he could have kicked his own ass for being the reason she cried.

"It's all right, Sasha." He gently wiped a tear from the corner of her eye then, brushing her trembling lips with his, added, "Just a little more and the discomfort will start to ease."

It ripped him apart to see another tear slide down the side of her cheek as he pushed forward and completely buried himself in her moist heat. His reflexes urged him to move, to thrust into her and complete the act of loving her, but he remained perfectly still. Her body needed time to adjust to his and he wasn't about to hurt her any more than he already had.

Gathering her close, he kissed away her tears. "No more pain, sweetheart. I promise."

"It's not really that bad," she said, taking a shuddering breath.

"I just wish that you'd let me know." He nuzzled the soft, wispy curls at her temple. "I might have been able to do something to make my entry a little less painful."

"You were so gentle, I don't see how you could have made it any easier," she murmured shyly. "And I did try to tell you."

He frowned. "When?"

Her watery smile did strange things to his insides. "Just before you assured me our lovemaking was not going to be a one-night stand."

He vaguely remembered her telling him there was something that she'd never done, but he'd thought she was going to tell him she'd never been one to engage in casual sex. That was when he'd jumped the gun and interrupted her to voice his assurance that wasn't what he wanted from her. Apparently, he'd made assumptions that were completely off the mark.

But as he continued to stare down at her lovely face, Blake knew as surely as he knew his own name that he meant what he'd said. His seduction of Sasha Kilgore might have started out as an attempt to even a score with his brother, but within the past thirty-six hours his focus had changed and he had no intention of limiting their lovemaking to this one night.

As he felt her begin to relax and accept him as part of her, the strain of holding himself in check became almost unbearable. He needed to love her, to bring her pleasure and find his own in the softness of her sweet body.

"I'm going to make love to you now, Sasha," he said, kissing her slightly parted lips.

He slowly pulled back, then eased forward as he

watched for any sign that he might be causing her discomfort. When he found none, he set an easy pace and in no time he felt her begin to respond, to tentatively move in unison with him.

But all too soon, he felt her tighten around him and he knew she was close to finding the release they both sought. Deepening his strokes, Blake had to grit his teeth to keep himself from unleashing the full force of his need. He was determined to insure Sasha's pleasure ahead of his own, even if it killed him. And as urgent as his need was, it just might.

When Sasha cried his name and he felt her tiny feminine muscles cling to him, then begin to rhythmically contract, he gave in to the demands of his body and thrust into her one final time. His body stiffened and the white-hot light of completion clouded his mind as he gave up his essence and emptied himself deep inside of her.

Drained of every ounce of energy he possessed, he collapsed on top of her and buried his face in the soft cloud of her auburn hair. "Are you all right, sweetheart?"

"That was…the most incredible experience…of my life," she said breathlessly.

Finally summoning enough strength to move to her side, Blake gathered her to him and held her close. "*You* were incredible."

"Is making love always like that?" she whispered, her breath soft against his heated skin.

He hesitated as he tried to put into words what he didn't fully understand himself. He'd found his pleasure with more women than he cared to admit—all of them light-years ahead of her in experience. But nothing could have prepared him for the degree of satisfaction he'd found with Sasha.

Unwilling to admit, even to himself, that what they'd shared was significant and unlike anything that had ever happened to him, he ignored her question in favor of one of his own. "After all this time of waiting to give your virginity to a man, why did you choose me, Sasha?"

"It's absolutely insane and you probably wouldn't believe me anyway," she answered, placing her warm palm on his bare chest.

He liked the way her touch felt on his skin and he covered her hand with his to hold it there. "Why don't you tell me and see if I believe you."

Her sigh feathered over his shoulder and sent an awakening wave of heat straight to his groin. "They weren't you."

She spoke so softly that he wasn't entirely certain he hadn't imagined her confession. "You saved yourself for me?" he asked incredulously.

Raising her head, she met his questioning gaze

directly. "It wasn't a conscious decision to wait for you, but I think I fell in love with you the first time I saw you back in high school. Since then, I've compared every one of my boyfriends to you and found them lacking in one way or another."

"Even Creed?"

"How many times do I have to tell you? Creed and I are just good friends." When she started to get out of bed, he held her to him. "Creed asked me to accompany him to social functions in order to discourage some the more persistent women looking for a great catch. There was never anything more to it than that."

Blake knew all too well the lengths some women would go to in their quest to catch a man with money and social status. "So you were helping him fend off the gold diggers?"

"Yes."

"And you never entertained the thought of becoming romantically involved with him?" Blake asked, needing to know.

She shook her head. "He wasn't you."

The clarity in her guileless green eyes verified her claim and rendered him absolutely speechless. From the moment he was born, he'd been compared to his older brothers and always seemed to fall just short of everyone's expectations. Even his father, the high and mighty Nash Fortune, had held him up to Case and Creed's achievements, both personally and professionally. But for the first time in his life, someone had compared him to one of his older brothers and Blake hadn't come up second-best.

As he continued to gaze at Sasha, a feeling like nothing he'd ever known filled his chest. For reasons he didn't dare contemplate, he never wanted to let her down, never wanted her to find him lacking in any way. Nor did he ever want another man touching her.

The sudden desire to brand her with his kiss became an undeniable need and Blake didn't think twice about pulling her beneath him to once again claim her sweet body for his own. She was his now and he had no intention of ever letting her forget it.

When Sasha went into work on Monday afternoon, she wasn't at all surprised to find Creed standing in her doorway less than five minutes after her arrival. To anyone else his demeanor would probably appear casual and unperturbed. But in the past year, Sasha had come to know him too well. He definitely had something on his mind and unless he'd undergone a radical personality change in the past few days, he was there to let her know exactly what it was.

"Did you enjoy your weekend in Deadwood?" he asked, walking over to ease himself down into the chair in front of her desk. His question was innocent enough and his tone casual, but she knew it was Creed's way of diplomatically bringing up the subject of her time with Blake.

"It was nice to get away for a while," she said, careful to keep her own tone as neutral as possible. Aside from the fact that she didn't feel like listening to Creed's repeated warnings about Blake, it was none of his concern what she did or with whom. "I especially liked visiting some of the museums and learning more about the town's colorful history. It really is fascinating."

He stared at her for several long seconds before his eyes narrowed and he shook his head. "You fel' into his trap, didn't you?"

"I don't have the slightest notion what you'r talking about," she lied, averting her gaze.

"Damn." Creed rose to his feet and began t pace the length of her office. "I knew I should hav gone with you to keep that bastard from pulling a fast one." Stopping suddenly, he turned to face her. "Did you sleep with him?"

Angry with Creed for prying, as well as with herself for being so transparent, Sasha shook her head. "What I do on my own time is none of your business, Creed. And I don't appreciate being treated to the third degree. If you want to keep our friendship intact, you'll drop this right here and now."

He let loose with a creative curse. "You don't know him like I do, Sasha. He's just like his mother—selfish, opportunistic and trouble from the word go." He released a frustrated breath as he shook his head. "The son of a bitch will only end up hurting you and if it's within my power to prevent it from happening, I will."

Sighing, she leaned back in her chair as she continued to stare at her friend. "I appreciate your concern, Creed. But I'm a grown woman and perfectly capable of making my own decisions. I can take care of myself."

As if cognizant of the line he was about to cross with their friendship, he walked to the door, then turned back to face her. "I realize you think you know what you're doing. But becoming involved with Blake Fortune would be a huge mistake."

"That may be," she said, careful to keep her voice as even as her emotions would allow. "But it's my mistake to make, Creed. Not yours."

He looked as if he'd like to argue the point further, then giving her a short nod, he warned as he walked out, "Just be sure to watch yourself around him, Sasha."

Long after Creed had left her office, she continued to stare at the open doorway. She was having a difficult time believing that they'd been talking about the same man.

She'd spent the weekend with Blake and found him to be nothing like the man Creed described. If Blake was selfish, she hadn't seen it. With her, he'd been kind, caring and extremely attentive. Her body heated in a very interesting way as she remembered just how much attention he'd given her.

After learning that she'd come to his bed a virgin, he couldn't have been more gentle or understanding. He'd not only been sensitive to the tenderness of her body and her lack of experience, he'd assured her pleasure before his own. That certainly negated Creed's claim that Blake was self-centered.

And after watching him interact with his employees and guests, it was easy to see why he'd been so successful with his venture into the gaming industry. Although he demanded his employees give one hundred and ten percent to their jobs, he'd earned their loyalty and respect by asking nothing more of them than he was willing to give himself. That didn't sound like a man who took advantage of others.

As she sat there contemplating why Creed felt

the way he did about his brother, Blake entered her office and closed the door. Her heart skipped a beat at the sight of him and she couldn't believe how much she'd missed being with him in such a short time. After flying back to Sioux Falls together on his private jet that morning, they'd parted ways at the airport. And while she'd returned to work, Blake had gone to his family's estate to visit his sister, Skylar.

But something about his expression warned her that things might not have gone well. "Was everything all right at home?"

"I'm not sure." He walked around the desk, pulled her to her feet and kissed her until they both gasped for breath. Then sitting in her chair, he settled her on his lap. "I missed you."

"I missed you, too," she whispered, wrapping her arms around his neck.

They sat in contented silence for several long moments and she could tell he was troubled by something. "What happened?"

He shrugged one broad shoulder. "As usual, Dad and Patricia were off somewhere doing whatever retired couples do."

Nash Fortune had handed over the reins of his thriving enterprise to his oldest sons, Creed and Case, a couple of years before Sasha had come to work at Dakota Fortune. But she'd met the elder Fortune and his third wife on several occasions and marveled at how devoted they were to each other.

"They certainly seem to be making the most of his retirement," she agreed. "But what about Skylar? Wasn't she at home?"

Blake looked pensive as he nodded. "Yeah, but only in body."

"Excuse me?"

"She was there, but her mind was clearly somewhere else," he said, frowning. "I've never seen her so quiet."

Knowing Skylar Fortune from the social and family events she'd attended with Creed, Sasha found it hard to believe that the youngest of the Fortune siblings could be even more reserved than usual. "Do you think she might be ill?"

"I don't think so," he said thoughtfully. He chuckled. "If her appetite is any indication, she's as healthy as one of her horses. She's gained so much weight lately that you never see her in anything but baggy sweaters or sweatshirts."

"Do you know if she's been seeing someone?" Sasha asked.

He looked confused. "What does that have to do with anything?"

She smiled. Like most men, Blake didn't have

the slightest clue the effect a failed relationship could have on a woman. Or what it sometimes compelled her to do.

"Skylar might be nursing a broken heart." She kissed his lean cheek. "Nina in accounting told me that after her breakup with her fiancé, she gained twenty pounds in a month because she went home every night after work and ate a pint of double-fudge chocolate-chunk ice cream."

He was silent a moment before an understanding expression crossed his handsome features. "I do remember seeing Skylar and Zach Manning at Case's wedding reception a few months back. At the time, I didn't think much of it, but I think there was something going on between them."

"Isn't he from New Zealand?"

Blake nodded. "He and our cousin, Max, have partnered up to start a horse-breeding operation in Australia and they've been over here a couple of times to check out Skylar's program." He gave her a smile that caused an exciting little tingle to traverse the length of her body. "But I don't want to discuss Zach Manning, his plans to breed horses or the sorry state of my little sister's love life."

A spark of heat ignited deep in the pit of her belly as Sasha stared at the man she'd fallen in love with. "What do you want to discuss?" She feigned thoughtfulness. "World affairs? The state of the economy? The price of tea in China?"

"None of the above," he said. "In fact—" he brushed his lips over hers "—I prefer action over words."

When his mouth settled on hers, Sasha decided that she did, too. They could talk on the phone after he returned to Deadwood sometime tomorrow. Right now, she was in Blake's arms and from the promise in his heated kiss, having a conversation was the last thing either of them wanted.

"Let's go to your place," he suggested, pulling back to capture her gaze with his.

"I just got here," she said, feeling as if the temperature in the room had risen a good ten degrees. She could feel his rapidly changing body against her thigh and it was creating an answering heat in the most feminine part of her. "And I really should tie up some loose ends on a project from last week."

Groaning, he took a deep breath as he rested his forehead against hers. "I've always admired a strong work ethic, but right now, I'd have to say I think it's a pain."

She smiled, then gave him a quick kiss and rose to her feet. "I said I had a few things to take care of. I didn't say that it would take me the rest of the afternoon." Tugging on his hand, she urged him out of her chair. "I should be ready to leave in about an hour. Do you think you can find something to occupy your time until then?"

"I can't hang out here in your office with you?" he asked as he stood up and wrapped his arms around her waist to pull her to him.

She shook her head. "You're too much of a distraction."

"But I thought you liked the way I distract you," he teased.

Shivers of sheer delight skipped up her spine when he leaned close and whispered the many ways he'd distracted her over the weekend. "I—I do like the d-diversion." She paused and took a deep breath in an effort to steady her voice. "And the sooner you let me get back to work, the sooner we'll be able to leave and you can divert my attention again."

He gave her a quick kiss, then released her and walked to the door. "I'll be back in an hour. And sweetheart, when we get to your apartment, I'm going to show you just how much of a distraction I can be."

When Blake left Sasha's office, he headed straight for the empty conference room at the end of the hall. Holding her soft body against him, kissing her sweet lips and talking about various ways he intended to make love to her when they got to her place had him harder than the Rock of Gibraltar. And unless he found a place to cool off, and damned quick, he'd be the subject of office gossip for days.

Besides, after discussing the possible source of his sister's despondent mood with Sasha, he had an overseas phone call to make. He knew it was probably the middle of the night in New Zealand, but he didn't care. Zach Manning could haul his sorry butt out of bed and explain what was going on between himself and Skylar. And it had better be good.

Closing the door behind him, Blake walked straight to the telephone on the mahogany credenza at the back of the conference room and dialed the Dakota Fortune operator. After instructing the woman to place his call, he waited for the connection to go through.

A few moments later, a sleepy male voice answered after several rings. "What!?"

"Zach? Blake Fortune here."

"Do you know what time it is here?" Zach demanded, his New Zealand accent thickened by sleep.

"Since you're half a world away, it's probably the middle of the night," Blake said, not at all concerned by the man's obvious displeasure at being awakened from a sound sleep.

A guttural curse crackled over the long-distance line. "I assume this isn't a social call. What do you want, Fortune?"

"An explanation." Never one to mince words, Blake couldn't see any reason to do so now. "What happened between you and Skylar when you were here in February for Case's wedding?"

Dead silence reigned for several long seconds and Blake knew he'd discovered the reason behind his sister's withdrawal.

"Why do you ask?" Zach finally responded, sidestepping an explanation.

"She hasn't been herself for the past couple of months and I want to know the reason why."

"Is she all right?"

The concern Blake detected in the man's voice was genuine enough, but that did little to appease his building anger. "Something is bothering her and it's my guess that you're behind it. I also figure you know what that something is and will be able to rectify the situation."

"I'll speak with her," Zach assured him without hesitation.

"Consider yourself warned, Manning. I don't like seeing my sister hurt."

"I'll set things right with Skylar immediately," Zach promised. To his credit the man didn't sound nearly as irritated as when he'd first answered Blake's call. In fact, Zach sounded rather enthusiastic about getting in touch with her.

"See that you do," Blake said, hanging up the phone without bidding the man farewell.

With the matter of his sister's broken heart resolved, Blake smiled as he checked his watch. Sasha's hour was almost up and he had every intention of taking her to her apartment and distracting her until they both collapsed from exhaustion.

Six

Dressed in nothing but Blake's white shirt, Sasha stared into the freezer compartment of her small refrigerator. "What would you like for dinner?"

Blake walked up behind her, wrapped his arms around her and pulled her back against him to kiss the side of her neck. "You'll do just fine."

She laughed as a familiar heat began to flow through her. "You have a one-track mind, Mr. Fortune."

"I can't help it." He tugged the collar of his shirt from her shoulder to allow him better access, and the feel of his firm lips on her sensitive skin sent tiny electric impulses skittering over every nerve in her body. "You bring out the best in me, sweetheart."

"More like the beast," she said, turning to face him.

When they'd arrived at her apartment, she'd barely managed to close and lock the door before Blake had them both stripped of their clothes and had carried her into the bedroom. That had been several hours ago and the passion arcing between them was every bit as strong now as it had been earlier in the day.

His sexy grin caused a familiar fluttering in the pit of her stomach. "If I remember correctly, you weren't exactly complaining when I—"

She placed her index finger to his lips. "Point taken," she said, blushing furiously.

His deep chuckle vibrated against her chest and caused the most interesting tingling in the tips of her breasts. "I love seeing you blush."

"That's apparent." She circled his bare shoulders with her arms and threaded her fingers in the dark blond hair at the nape of his neck. "You've been making me turn as red as a lobster all afternoon."

"That wasn't embarrassment, Sasha. That was the blush of desire."

As if to prove his point, he pressed his lower

body closer and the feel of his strong arousal against her lower belly caused her to go warm all over. "If you keep this up—"

"Interesting choice of words," he said, sliding his hands down to cup her bottom and pull her even closer. "As I'm sure you can tell, that's not a problem."

She gasped from the waves of renewed need that flowed through her when she felt the strength of his arousal against her lower belly. "We're never going to find time to go over my ideas for your promotional campaign."

He kissed her collarbone, then began to unbutton his shirt to nibble at every new inch he exposed. "Is that what you really want to do right now?"

When he parted the garment and covered her breasts with his hands, her knees began to wobble and her heart pounded so hard against her ribs, she felt as if she'd run a marathon. "Wh-what was the question again?"

"Damned if I know," he said as he lowered his head to take her nipple into his mouth.

Teasing her relentlessly, Sasha wasn't at all surprised to feel a delicious need begin to tighten her womb. After making love the entire afternoon, how could they possibly be hungrier for each other now than before?

"This…is insane."

He raised his head and the intensity in the depths of his eyes, the sparkle of heat, told her in no uncertain terms what he wanted. "We're about to go crazy together, sweetheart."

Fully expecting him to pick her up and carry her back into the bedroom, she tightened her arms around him in surprise when he lifted her to sit on the edge of the counter. "Wh-what are you doing?"

"I want you here." Buttons skittered across the tiled floor when he jerked the lapels of his shirt open the rest of the way to give him better access to her body. Then, shoving his boxer briefs to his ankles, he entered her in one smooth stroke. "Now."

The feel of him filling her completely, the heat that threatened to consume her when he began to rhythmically thrust into her and the fact that they were making love somewhere other than the bedroom heightened her excitement in ways she could have never imagined. The urgency arcing between them was more powerful than ever before and Sasha felt as if she would burst into flames at any moment.

Tightening her legs around his slim hips, she clung to him as he relentlessly built the ache of unfulfilled desire within her. All too quickly his body demanded that she give into their fiery passion and she gladly complied as bursts of pleasure shook her to the core.

As she trembled against him, she felt the slight swelling of his body within hers a moment before the moist heat of his release filled her. As she held him to her, tears burned at her tightly closed eyes from the beauty of what they'd shared.

If she'd had any lingering doubts about her feelings for him being the remnants of the schoolgirl's crush, they had just dissipated like mist under a warm summer sun. She loved him with a woman's heart and belonged to him, body and soul. And no matter what the future held for them, that would never change.

"You want me to do what?" Blake couldn't believe what Sasha was proposing.

"I'd like for you to consider doing a television commercial for the grand opening of Fortune's Gold," she said patiently.

"I have no objections to the concept of buying airtime to run commercials for my hotels and casinos," he said, shaking his head. "I do, however, have a huge problem with starring in the damned things."

Sitting cross-legged in the middle of her bed, wearing nothing but his buttonless shirt and a sweet smile, she looked so sexy and desirable, Blake had to force himself to remember that he'd promised to listen to her ideas for his ad campaign. But if anything could bring him back to reality with a resounding thump, it was the thought of going in front of a TV camera. Just the idea caused a knot in his stomach.

"Blake, you're the natural choice," she insisted. "You're not only the owner of the Fortune Casino Corporation, your enthusiasm and sincerity when you encourage people to visit your establishments will be captured and add a great deal to your advertising. It will make the viewers feel as if you're issuing a personal invitation."

He understood what she was saying and the value of the visual media. But the thought of following the nightly news like some monkey in a sideshow, even for the fifteen to thirty seconds the commercials would run, made him want take off for parts unknown.

"I think a professional actor would be a better choice," he said, leaning back against the pillows.

"I don't." Raising up on her hands and knees, she crawled across the bed to hover over him. "You're handsome." She kissed his chin. "Sexy." She traced the outline of his lips with her tongue. "And you'll have the women flocking to your casinos in droves."

He pulled her beneath the sheet that covered

him from the waist down, then turned to his side and aligned their bodies so they were facing each other. "You really think I'm handsome and sexy?" he asked, slipping his hand beneath the shirt to caress her satiny skin.

"Don't change the subject," she said, sounding less than convincing. "I'm trying to have a serious conversation with you about the marketing strategy for the Fortune Casino Corporation."

Slowly sliding his hand down her thigh, he smiled when her eyes fluttered shut and she sighed softly. "Do you really want to discuss business now?"

"We should."

"Who are you trying to convince, Sasha? Me or yourself?"

When she opened her eyes, the sparkle of desire in her emerald gaze caused his body to harden so fast it left him feeling light-headed. "We're never going to get anything done if you keep distracting me all the time," she complained.

He moved his hand lower to find her receptive and ready for him. "Oh, I think we've accomplished quite a bit."

She poked him in his ribs. "I wasn't talking about our lovemaking."

"That's a shame," he said, kissing his way from her shoulder, down the valley between her breasts to the small indentation of her navel. "You've inspired me more than I ever thought possible and I'm enjoying finding new ways to love you."

"Your creativity certainly has…been working overtime."

The hitch in her voice was an indication of her heightening excitement and, determined to imprint himself in her mind and on her soul, Blake turned her to her back. He held her gaze with his as he moved to kneel between her legs and he knew the exact moment she realized his intention.

"B-Blake, you can't—"

"Yes, I can." He could tell that she was embarrassed by the thought of what he was about to do. "I'm going to give you the most intimate kiss a man can give a woman, Sasha. And when I'm finished, there won't be a doubt left in your mind that you've been loved as thoroughly and completely as it's within my power to do."

Unwilling to allow her to protest further, Blake bent to give to her as he'd never given to any woman and when he kissed her deeply, her soft sighs quickly turned to passionate moans. Her slender body trembled, then suddenly bucked against him and he knew the intense pleasure was about to overtake her.

Relentless in his effort to bring her to the brink,

he smiled from the satisfaction of hearing her cry out his name as the tension released her from its tight hold and she found the ecstasy of her fulfillment. Only then did he move to lie by her side, his chest filling with indescribable tenderness when he realized that she'd drifted off into a peaceful, sated sleep.

As he held Sasha close, Blake stared at the ceiling and mentally reviewed everything that had taken place over the past few days. He wasn't the least bit proud of himself for planning to seduce her as a way to even the score with his brother. Aside from the fact that she and Creed had never been romantically involved, Blake knew now that Sasha was the only one who stood to be hurt in his game of revenge.

He took a deep breath as a wave of guilt threatened to swamp him. She could never learn the truth behind his sudden interest in her after all this time. If she did, the knowledge would crush her. And he'd rather cut out his own heart than ever let that happen.

When he glanced down at her beautiful face pillowed on his shoulder, an emotion that scared the living hell out of him filled every fiber of his being. He knew that they were good together, that he felt more alive and content in her presence than he'd ever felt in his life. But he refused to acknowledge there was anything more to it than two people finding companionship and pleasure in each others' arms.

Satisfied that he'd found an explanation for the unwarranted feeling, he kissed the top of her head. They would continue to see each other until one or both of them lost interest. Then, when the time came for them to part ways, they would do so as good friends who could look back on their time together with deep fondness and no regrets.

Sasha watched the production crew test the lighting and do a sound check in the lobby of Fortune's Gold as they prepared to film the last segment of the commercials for Blake's casinos. She'd finally managed to talk him into being his own spokesman for the ad campaign, but it certainly hadn't been easy. He'd come up with every excuse imaginable, from claiming that he would feel like he was on display to wanting to maintain his anonymity. But in the end, she'd convinced him by showing him the marketing statistics. It had been proven time and again that when the public felt a personal rapport with the owner of an establishment, the amount of traffic increased and ultimately so did profits.

"We're ready for Mr. Fortune as soon as Sally

Ann finishes his makeup," the director said, walking over to stand beside Sasha.

She'd worked with Michael Atkinson on several campaigns for Dakota Fortune and knew his production company was the best in Sioux Falls. By the time the commercials aired in all of the major cities across the Midwest, he would have them edited and tweaked to show Blake and the Fortune Casino Corporation in the best possible light.

"I want to thank you for working this into your busy schedule, Michael." With a little less than two weeks left before the opening of Fortune's Gold, she'd had to scramble to get Michael's company to shoot the commercials, as well as arrange scheduling with all of the television stations to run them on such short notice.

"It's been well worth it, Ms. Kilgore." Michael grinned. "It's not every day that my crew and I get to fly to a shoot on a private jet or have our lunches catered by a master chef."

"Mr. Fortune appreciates your willingness to put your other clients on hold in order to shoot his commercial," she said, diplomatically ignoring the fact that Blake was paying the man double his normal rate to expedite the job.

"Let's get this spectacle over with," Blake groused as he removed the tissues the makeup artist had tucked into his collar to keep from discoloring his shirt.

Once Michael moved away to have a final word with the cameraman, Blake leaned close to whisper in Sasha's ear. "I'm going to get even with you for this."

As he described exactly how he intended to make her pay up, a tingling sensation coursed through her. She started to tell him that she was looking forward to her night of reckoning, but Michael chose that moment to motion for Blake to step in front of the camera, and for the next hour she watched him deliver the ad copy she'd helped him put together.

At first, Blake appeared stiff and extremely uncomfortable. He glanced her way several times and she could tell he was adding to the sensual retribution he had planned for her. But by the last few takes, he appeared confident and completely at ease in front of the camera.

When Michael announced the job was a wrap and he and his crew began tearing down their equipment, Sasha smiled as she walked over to Blake. "That wasn't all that unpleasant, was it?"

Placing his hand to the small of her back, he guided her toward the casino exit. "No, it wasn't as bad as I figured it would be. But I sure as hell don't plan on repeating the experience."

Sasha stopped when she saw Blake's limo waiting outside and realized that he meant for them to leave. "I should probably stay until Michael—"

"I have people to see that Atkinson and his crew get packed up and on their way." He waited for her to get into the limousine, then slid in beside her. With a look that sent her blood pressure soaring, he pushed the button to raise the privacy screen between them and the driver.

"You owe me big time," he said, dragging her onto his lap. "And guess what?"

She laughed when his fingers danced over her ticklish ribs. "What?"

"It's payday, sweetheart."

"Plan on spending the entire week of the grand opening here in Deadwood with me."

Wrapped in plush hotel robes, Sasha and Blake snuggled on his couch as they stared at the flames from the gas log in the fireplace. "I would love to, but unfortunately, I can't take that much time off."

"Why not?"

A wave of goose bumps covered her arms when he kissed the side of her neck and she had to concentrate hard in order to give him a coherent answer. "I have to pay rent, utilities and eat. I can't do either if I don't work."

"Don't worry about it, sweetheart. I'll see to it that—"

"Don't you dare say you'll pay my bills for me." She pulled back to let him see that she meant what she said. "I have never taken money from anyone that I didn't earn and I'm not about to start now."

He shook his head. "Calm down, Sasha. I was going to tell you that I would arrange for you to have the time away from Dakota Fortune with pay."

It was her turn to shake her head. "I can't let you do that."

"Why not?"

From his baffled expression, she could tell he didn't have an inkling as to why she felt the need to refuse. "For one thing, it wouldn't be fair to my coworkers. They work just as hard as I do and they won't be offered time off with pay."

A deep scowl creased his forehead. "Why are you being so stubborn about this?"

"Because it doesn't sit well with me." Trying a different tack, she asked, "Would you pay one of your employees for work they didn't do?"

"No." There wasn't a bit of hesitation in his answer.

"Then why would you think it was all right to do it for me?"

He surprised her when he smiled and shook his

head. "You're wrong, sweetheart. I wouldn't be paying you for nothing."

It was her turn to feel confused. "Would you care to explain?"

"How many hours would you say you've put in on my ad campaign and how many strings did you have to pull to make it all happen?" he asked, catching her hand in his to tug her back down beside him.

She shrugged as she settled back against him. "I don't know. I haven't kept track."

"You worked last weekend to come up with a plan and every night I've called this past week, you've been ironing out the details." He kissed the top of her head. "And correct me if I'm wrong, but I don't remember giving you a single dime for any of it."

She was beginning to understand his reasoning, but that hadn't been part of their agreement. "I don't expect you to pay me. You asked me to do a favor for you as a friend. Which I did."

His frustrated breath stirred the curls at her temple. "All right. I appreciate your efforts and accept that you won't let me compensate you for your time." He wrapped his arms around her and held her close as he pushed her robe aside to trail kisses down the column of her neck and over her shoulder. "But I'm not asking you to be with me for opening week as a favor. As your boss, I'm telling you to be here."

"You can't do that." Desire began to stir within her as his lips continued to move over her skin. But she refused to give in to it. They were having a difference of opinion and she wasn't going to let him distract her until they got it settled once and for all.

"Sure I can." He laid her down on the couch cushions, parted her robe and leaned to kiss his way down the slope of her breast. "I'm the boss. Remember?"

"But—"

"I'll arrange for you to work here opening week, instead of at the Dakota Fortune offices." He took her puckered nipple into his mouth and drew on it deeply, causing ribbons of warmth to swirl to the very core of her. When he raised his head, he asked, "Now, do you have anymore questions, sweetheart?"

"None," she answered, shaking her head. "None at all."

Seven

As Blake and his managers stood in front of Fortune's Gold for the ribbon-cutting ceremony officially opening his newest casino, he scanned the crowd waiting to enter Deadwood's most elaborate hotel. Asking for Sasha's help had certainly paid off. There were twice as many people gathered to try out the gaming tables and slot machines than there had been at either of the openings for his other casinos.

Searching to find her in the sea of people, when he spotted her standing over to the side with a distinguished-looking gentlemen, Blake barely managed to contain his shock. She was exchanging polite conversation with his father, the all powerful Nash Fortune.

Why was he here? He'd hadn't bothered to attend the openings for Belle of Fortune or Lucky Fortune. In fact, his father hadn't visited Deadwood in the six years that Blake had lived here.

But more surprising than having his father in attendance was the fact that Nash was alone. Where was Patricia? His father and stepmother had been inseparable since Nash's retirement and the fact that she wasn't at his side was quite significant.

But Blake didn't have time to speculate about the absence of his stepmother. He had to deliver a short speech, then participate in the cutting of the wide red ribbon officially opening the doors to Fortune's Gold for business.

As happened with the grand openings for his other two hotel casinos, Blake's position as the owner of Fortune Casino Corporation required that he not only preside over the ceremony, but that he be available to greet guests and endure being interviewed by several newspaper and television reporters. Fortunately, it only took a couple of hours for the patrons to settle into their games of choice and the media to move on to whatever else they deemed newsworthy for the day.

Finally free to go in search of Sasha, he found her in the coffee shop seated at a table with his father. Blake's heart lurched when their eyes met. She was, without a doubt, the most beautiful, alluring woman he'd ever met.

"Everything seemed to go quite well," she said when he walked over to join them.

"I'm fairly pleased with the way things went." Unconcerned that his father was watching, Blake kissed her sweet lips, then lowered himself into the chair beside her. "But I'm glad it's over."

"I always hated having to preside over things like this," Nash said, nodding.

A waitress appeared, seemingly out of nowhere to place a cup of coffee in front of Blake. When she moved away, he turned his attention to his father and stuck out his hand in a more formal greeting. "I didn't expect to see you here, Dad."

His father cleared his throat as they shook hands and if he didn't know better, Blake would have sworn that Nash looked a little chagrined. "I thought it was time to see what's claimed my youngest son's attention for the past several years."

An uncomfortable silence followed his father's telling statement. They both knew that Nash had never paid much attention to Blake, nor had he lifted a finger to stop his two oldest sons from pushing Blake out of Dakota Fortune after he'd retired. Then, when Blake had announced he was going to try his hand at the gaming industry, Nash had dismissed it as a waste of time and hadn't seemed to care one way or the other how his youngest son fared with the venture.

"If you two gentlemen will excuse me, I think I'd like to try my luck at the slot machines," Sasha said, picking up her purse.

Blake knew she was leaving in order to give them the privacy to work through their differences. But he didn't hold out much hope of that ever happening. His entire life, he'd tried to measure up to his father's expectations and all he'd received for his efforts was to be compared with his older brothers, Case and Creed. In his father's eyes, Blake always came up lacking.

When Sasha rose to her feet to make her exit, both he and his father stood up. "It was nice seeing you again, Mr. Fortune," she said as she politely shook Nash's hand.

"It was my pleasure, Sasha."

"I'll see you a bit later, Blake." She placed her hand on his arm and gave him an understanding smile. "After you and your father catch up."

"I'll find you," he promised.

As she walked away, he and his father both watched her leave.

"She's a very lovely girl and a delight to be around," Nash said, sitting back down. "She's highly intelligent, too."

"Yes, she is," Blake agreed as he settled into his chair. "She's directly responsible for the day being a complete success."

"Creed speaks very highly of her," his father added. "He says she's done an excellent job in the PR department at Dakota Fortune."

"I'm sure he does think she's quite good at her job," Blake said tightly. He and his father had never had a conversation in which one of his older brothers wasn't mentioned. The sad thing was he doubted his father even realized how it made Blake feel.

They both fell silent for several moments before Blake finally let go of his irritation and thought to ask "Where's Patricia?"

Nash sighed heavily and Blake could tell he was deeply troubled. "She planned on coming with me, but backed out at the last minute."

"That doesn't sound like her. Wasn't she feeling well?" Patricia Blackstone Fortune had been more of a mother to Blake than his own mother ever had and he was genuinely concerned for her well-being.

"I'm not sure." A worried expression marred his father's distinguished features. "Something's been upsetting her lately and I can't think of what it could be."

"Have you talked to her about what's wrong?" Blake asked as he motioned for the waitress to refill their coffee cups.

Nash waited for the woman to walk away before he nodded. "I've asked her several times, but she won't tell me."

Blake frowned. "That doesn't sound like Patricia."

"No, it doesn't." His father hesitated a moment before giving Blake a meaningful look. "I do have a theory though."

"What is it?"

Nash met his questioning gaze head-on. "I think it might have something to do with Trina."

At the mention of his mother's name, a tight knot formed in the pit of Blake's stomach. "What makes you think Trina has anything to do with Patricia being upset?"

"You know how she is," Nash said, shaking his head. "She thrives on upsetting others and if she's not stirring up some kind of trouble or meddling in someone's life, she's not happy."

"But that doesn't mean she's involved in what's bothering Patricia," Blake said evenly.

Trina Watters Fortune was difficult at the best of times and at her worst, a vindictive, unreasonable shrew. But she was still his mother and Blake felt a certain obligation to defend her.

"It didn't even occur to me to suspect that she was until I saw Patricia's reaction when Ivy mentioned Trina's name in passing." Nash lifted his cup and, staring at Blake over the rim, added, "Patricia turned white as a sheet and had to leave the room."

Ivy Woodhouse had been the family's chef as long as Blake could remember, but for reasons he couldn't explain, there was something about the woman that he'd never liked. "What did Ivy say about Trina?"

"It wasn't what she said—it was Trina's name that sent Patricia into a tailspin." Nash set his cup back down on the table and shook his head. "You still have contact with Trina, don't you?"

"Some," Blake admitted slowly.

"Do you think she's behind whatever is wrong with Patricia?" Nash asked point-blank.

Blake started to tell his father that Trina couldn't possibly be responsible for everything that had gone wrong in Nash's life, but stopping himself, he gave his father a meaningful look. "Ever since you threw Trina out for cheating on you and divorced her, I've been listening to you blame her for everything that's gone wrong in our family."

"She's a—"

Blake held up his hand to stop his father. "And on the other hand, whenever I'm around Trina, I have to listen to her tirade about how you ruined her life and how unfair you were to her. And I'm sick and tired of it."

Nash looked taken aback. "I didn't realize—"

"That's because from the time you and Trina split, you've both been too busy using me as a pawn in your little game of revenge and one-upmanship," Blake interrupted. "When I was younger, each time it was Trina's weekend for visitation, I got the third degree about what was going on at home—what you were doing and who you were seeing. Then when I returned to the estate, when you weren't telling me I should be more like Case and Creed, I had to listen to you complain about what a gold digger Trina is and how she tricked you into marrying her after the death of your father."

They were silent for some time before Nash finally spoke. "I understand the position we've put you in. It couldn't have been easy for you or Skylar." Nash wasn't offering an apology, but then Blake hadn't expected him to.

"I survived," Blake said, finally shedding the feeling of being torn between his parents.

His father nodded. "I'd say you not only

survived, but you've done quite well for yourself, son. You've accomplished quite a bit since leaving Dakota Fortune, and you've made quite a name for yourself without my backing." Nash's voice turned gruff. "I'm proud of you, son."

In that moment, Blake felt closer to his father than he ever had. "Thanks, Dad. That means a lot coming from you."

Nash drew a deep breath, scooted his chair back and stood up. "Well, I think I'd better get back to Sioux Falls to see about Patricia."

Blake rose to his feet to walk out of the coffee shop with his father. "Now that you've checked out my operation, you and Patricia will have to come back and spend a little time here in Deadwood."

"We'll do that," his father said, shaking Blake's hand.

"Give Patricia my best."

Nodding, Nash walked out of the hotel and climbed into the back of a waiting limousine.

Stuffing his hands in the front pockets of his suit pants, emotion filled Blake's chest as he watched the long black car pull from beneath the covered entryway and disappear down the circular drive. For the first time in his life, Nash had acknowledged Blake's accomplishments without comparing him to his older brothers…and it felt good.

Perhaps this was the first step in forging a new relationship between father and son.

"Blake, have you seen today's newspaper from Sioux Falls?"

Propped up against the pillows on his bed, Sasha had chosen to read while he watched a baseball game on television. But in retrospect, she wished she'd opted for a nap. Dreaming, even if it had been a nightmare, would have been a lot less disturbing than what she'd just read.

He shook his head without looking up from the game. "No, why? Did they mention something about the opening of Fortune's Gold?"

"You might say that."

Something in her tone must have tipped him off that she was far from pleased with what she'd read because he turned his head to give her a questioning look. "What did they say?"

She pointed to the society column as she handed him the newspaper. "See for yourself."

His graphic curse reverberated around the room the moment he saw the pictures and read the caption. "Where the hell did this gossip monger come up with her information? And who took these pictures?"

"Your guess is as good as mine." Too upset to sit

still, she got out of bed and began to pace the length of his bedroom. "I know we haven't been trying to hide the fact that we're seeing each other. But I certainly didn't expect to see not one, but two pictures of me in the newspaper with a headline that reads Social Climber Sasha Kilgore Ditches One Fortune Brother in Favor of Another."

"The picture of me kissing you was taken in the coffee shop the day of the grand opening," he said, studying the image.

"And the one of Creed dancing with me was taken at Case and Gina's wedding reception in February." She shook her head. "But I don't find the pictures as upsetting as what the columnist wrote about me. She portrays me as a social mercenary trying to play one brother against the other." Thoroughly miserable, tears filled her eyes as she turned to look at him. "That's not me. That's not who I am."

"I know, sweetheart." Blake tossed the newspaper aside, got out of bed and walked over to pull her into his arms. "Anyone who knows you won't believe a word of it."

"But there are thousands of readers who don't know me and they—"

"Aren't important," he said, sliding his hands up and down her back in a soothing manner. "We know the truth and that's all that matters."

As his tender touch chased away some of her tension, she wrapped her arms around his waist and leaned against his solid support. "I suppose you're right. But I can't understand why the columnist had to be so vindictive in the way she reported the story. It's almost like she's trying to use me to widen the rift between you and Creed."

"Scandals sell newspapers, Sasha." His chest rose and fell against her as he took a deep breath. "I was too young to pay much attention at the time, but I've been told that when my parents divorced, newspaper circulation went way up in Sioux Falls."

"Having the details of their breakup being made the talk of the town must have been extremely painful for your family," she said, wondering why the media couldn't respect the privacy of others.

"I'm sure it was for my father, but Trina probably enjoyed the hell out of it. She thrives on things like that."

Sasha leaned back to look up at him. "Why would your mother want to have information like that reported for all to see?"

He rested his forehead against hers. "If you knew her, you wouldn't be asking that question. She's one of a kind. And believe me, sweetheart, that's a real blessing."

Sasha didn't know what to say. She remembered

Creed telling her that Blake's mother was bad news, but she'd thought he'd been exaggerating because of the hard feelings he had for Blake. Apparently, she'd thought wrong.

"But I don't want talk about her, slanderous newspaper columnists or those clueless people with nothing better to do than believe a pack of lies." He kissed the tip of her nose. "I have other, more enjoyable ways to spend our time."

"What did you have in mind?" she asked as he hooked his finger in the spaghetti strap of her satin nightgown.

"Come back to bed and it'll be my pleasure to show you, sweetheart."

Blake held Sasha close as he watched the shadows of night gradually be chased away by the first light of dawn. After they'd made love, she'd drifted off, but sleep had escaped him.

He'd been more bothered by the newspaper article that he'd let on to Sasha. But not for himself. She was the one whose reputation was being called into question. And that's what caused the anger burning deep in his belly.

Blake had long ago gotten used to being fodder for the gossip columnists. Whether any of the Fortunes liked it or not, it went hand in hand with being a member of the wealthiest family in South Dakota. But Sasha wasn't used to having her private life chronicled for the masses to read about over their morning coffee.

Her name had appeared in the newspaper a few times because of the social functions and charity events she and Creed had attended together, but those stories hadn't been based on speculation or been malicious in tone. The article in yesterday's paper had been both and read more like something Trina would write than a reputable columnist.

He closed his eyes in an effort to block out the truth. His half siblings, Case and Eliza, and even his Australian cousin, Max, had had information about them leaked to the press and they'd all accused Trina of being behind it. But surely she wouldn't do the same thing to her own son. Would she?

Blake wasn't so sure. But the next time he stopped by her place for a visit, he had every intention of finding out.

Eight

"Do you have a minute?"

Sasha was surprised, not only by Creed's question, but the fact that he'd even asked it. He never cared how busy she was or what she was doing. If he wanted to drop by her office to chat, he walked right on in. Of course, as co-president of Dakota Fortune, he was her boss and entitled to do that.

"Sure, what do you need?"

An ominous feeling filled her when he held up a news clipping as he reached to close her office door. "We need to talk."

"That's the gossip column that ran in last weekend's newspaper, isn't it?" she asked, wondering if the nefarious story would ever go away.

"Yes." Creed had been out of town on business for the past six days and had apparently just learned about the article.

Walking over to her desk, he slapped the clipping down in front of her. She gasped when she read the sticky note attached to it. "How does it feel to come out the loser for a change?" She looked up at him. "Where did you get this?"

"It arrived in today's mail."

She felt as if she might be sick. "Who would do such a thing?"

"I think we both know who's responsible," he growled.

"Y-you think Blake sent this to you?"

"Who else?"

"You're wrong, Creed." Sasha's fingers trembled as she rubbed at her suddenly throbbing temples. "Blake would never do anything like this."

He propped his fists on the surface of her desk, then leaned forward. "Are you sure?"

Tears filled her eyes as she nodded. "Of course."

"Then who else would be malicious enough to send me something like this?"

"I don't know." She felt as if she were being

interrogated on a witness stand and Creed was her prosecutor, judge and jury.

When she opened her bottom desk drawer for a tissue, then wiped at an errant tear on her cheek, Creed swore vehemently. "I knew he'd do something like this. I just didn't anticipate it happening this soon."

"Y-you're wrong, Creed." Sasha tried to sniff back a fresh wave of tears. "Blake's not like that. What would he have to gain?"

"The satisfaction of publicly humiliating me," Creed stated flatly. "Sending this to me was just his way of rubbing my nose in it."

She couldn't believe what she was hearing. Other than the picture of her and Creed dancing at Case and Gina's wedding reception, his name had only been mentioned a couple of times. She'd been the one the columnist had focused on.

"You think you've been publicly humiliated? How do you think I feel?" she asked, suddenly more angry than hurt. "I'm the one who's been accused of being a social-climbing gold digger."

That seemed to drain away much of his anger and, straightening to his full height, he shook his head. "I never meant to dismiss the effect this has had on you, Sasha."

"But that's exactly what you've just done," she said, saddened that her friend hadn't even considered how the story might have upset her.

They stared silently at each other for what seemed like an eternity, each knowing their friendship had suffered a serious blow.

"Are you going to Deadwood this evening?" he finally asked.

She shook her head. "Blake's flying in later this afternoon to spend the weekend here."

Creed's mouth flattened into a tight line a moment before he nodded, and without another word walked out of her office.

Feeling drained from the confrontation, Sasha began to carefully stack the marketing charts she'd been working on when Creed had shown up. After what he'd just put her through, he owed her the rest of the afternoon off. With pay.

As she retrieved her purse from the bottom drawer of her desk, turned off her computer and left her office, she made a conscious decision not to mention the disturbing incident to Blake. The brothers were already at odds and there was no way she was going to add fuel to a fire that was rapidly growing out of control. Nor was she going to be the catalyst that brought their feud to a head.

* * *

Getting into the shiny red sports car he kept at the airport for his frequent visits to Sioux Falls, Blake started the powerful engine and headed straight for Sasha's apartment. It had been four days since she'd left Deadwood and he couldn't believe how much he'd missed her. He'd called her every night, but phone conversations were a poor substitute for holding her, kissing her and making love to her until they both collapsed from exhaustion.

A half hour later, when he parked the car in front of her apartment building and got out to walk up to her door, he whistled a tune. Life was good. Profits at his three casinos were higher than any of the projections; there hadn't been any more reports about him and Sasha in the gossip columns and he was going to spend the next three days with the most exciting woman he'd ever known. As far as he was concerned, it didn't get any better than that.

When he stopped to dig Sasha's apartment key from his jeans pocket, he smiled. She was going to be surprised and hopefully quite pleased when she came home from work and found that he'd had a caterer deliver a specially prepared dinner for them. She was expecting him to take her out, but after spending the past four days without her in his arms, the last place Blake wanted them to be was in a crowded restaurant.

"It's past time that you and I have it out, little brother."

At the sound of his brother's angry voice, Blake's good mood took a nosedive and he turned to find Creed storming up the sidewalk toward him. "I don't have anything to say to you."

"But I have plenty to say to you and you're going to listen."

"The hell I am." Blake wasn't the least bit intimidated by Creed's menacing expression. "I have plans for the evening and they don't include talking to you."

"I don't give a damn about you or your plans," Creed said, poking Blake in the chest with his index finger. "You're going to listen."

White hot fury invaded every fiber of Blake's being. "Do that again and I'll knock the hell out of you."

Although there were six years difference in their ages, they were pretty well matched in size and build. And if it came to blows, Blake figured he had a pretty good chance of taking Creed in a fight.

"Until today, I couldn't figure out why you'd taken a sudden interest in Sasha when you hadn't so much as given her a second glance in the four years she's worked at Dakota Fortune," Creed growled.

"And you think you've figured it out now?" Blake snapped back.

"Oh, yeah." Creed's smile was filled with loathing. "Because it appeared that Sasha and I were a couple, you decided to seduce her away from me. But you were too blinded by your jealousy of me to see that there was never anything romantic between us."

Guilt coursed through Blake. That was exactly the way his involvement with Sasha had started out. Fortunately, it hadn't taken long for him to realize how special she was and how much he needed her in his life.

But Blake's need to retaliate quickly became stronger than his sense of regret and before he could stop himself, he lashed out. "I figured that out about the same time I took her virginity."

Creed laughed humorlessly. "And she was ripe for the picking, wasn't she?"

"What's that supposed to mean?" Blake demanded, barely resisting the urge to plant his fist in his brother's nose.

"I've seen the way she looked at you over the past year. But being a self-absorbed bastard, I don't suppose you could see that she was attracted to you." Creed gave him a disgusted look. "Although for the life of me, I'll never understand why."

Blake shook his head. "I don't give a damn what you do or don't understand. Sasha's with me now and you're out of the picture." Without thinking, he added, "I win."

"A real man would walk away from this before Sasha ends up getting hurt." Creed raised an arrogant eyebrow. "But then, her feelings have never been your concern, have they? You were too focused on getting back at me to consider what your little game would do to her. And if the truth is known, you wouldn't have cared even if you had."

Blake didn't think he'd ever despised his brother more than he did at that moment. "I've never made a secret of the fact that I'll do whatever it takes just for the privilege of watching you land on your ass. But that's not—"

He started to tell Creed that he'd come to care too much for Sasha to hurt her in any way, but the words died in Blake's throat when he heard the soft female gasp behind him. Spinning around, Blake felt as if he was being torn apart when he saw the devastated expression on Sasha's sweet face and the tears streaming unchecked from her emerald eyes.

Neither he nor Creed had noticed her opening the apartment door, and Blake knew that she'd heard every one of the verbal barbs and accusations that they'd hurled at each other.

Arriving home from the office, Sasha had barely had time to change clothes and feed her cat, Melvin, before she'd heard the angry male voices outside of her apartment door. When she'd peeked out the window to see what was going on, the elation she'd felt at the sight of Blake had quickly turned to desolation. He and Creed had been embroiled in a heated argument and it hadn't taken long for her to realize that she was the subject of their battle.

"H-how could you?" she stammered, unsure which of the Fortune brothers to address first.

"Sasha—"

"Sweetheart—"

They both spoke at once, but she'd heard more than enough. "Don't." She shook her head. "There's nothing left to say."

Blake took a step toward her. "You heard—"

"E-everything," she said, drawing back. If he touched her, she knew for certain she'd shatter into a million pieces.

"I thought you were still at work," Creed said, his expression guarded.

"After our conversation, I didn't feel like staying at the office." She swiped at the tears running down her cheeks. "But don't trouble yourself with firing me for leaving work early."

"I wasn't going to," Creed said, frowning. "Why would you think that I would?"

"It doesn't matter whether you were or not because effective immediately, I'm no longer an employee of Dakota Fortune." When he opened his mouth as if he intended to refuse her resignation, she held up her hand. "I don't want to hear it. I thought you were my friend, Creed."

"I am," he insisted.

She shook her head. "A true friend wouldn't have talked to me the way you did earlier today."

"What did you say to her?" Blake demanded, his fists doubled at his sides.

"It doesn't matter," Sasha answered, staring at Creed. She feared she wouldn't be able to continue if she looked at Blake. And it was extremely important that she let them both know exactly what their feuding had cost them.

"I'm here defending you now," Creed said stubbornly. "If that's not friendship, I don't know what is."

"You weren't defending me as much as you were letting Blake know what easy prey you thought I was." She could tell that her statement shocked him, but it was past time they both heard just how destructive their warring had become and the high price they'd both have to pay for it. "In light of everything that's happened today, I think you'll have to agree that our friendship has come to an end, Creed."

"It's just as well, sweetheart," Blake interjected. "The son of a bitch wouldn't know how to be a friend if his life depended on it."

Sasha finally looked at him and she felt as if her heart broke all over again. "What you did to me is far worse than anything Creed could have ever done." Her voice caught on a sob. "Only the ones you love the most have the power to devastate you."

"Sasha, listen to me," Blake said, reaching for her.

"Don't touch me." She brushed his hand away. "Don't ever touch me again."

"Sasha, sweetheart, you don't mean that."

"Yes, I do." She took a deep breath as she forced herself to push the all-consuming emotional pain aside and dig deep within her soul to muster the last scrap of her tattered pride. "How could you have such little regard for my feelings? Did you even think of what it would do to me when I discovered that you were using me to get back at Creed?"

"If you'll let me explain—"

"I don't want to hear your excuses, Blake." She shook her head. "You win?" she quoted him. "I think that more than sums up the reasons behind your sudden interest in me, don't you?" Sasha held out her hand to Blake. "I'd like my apartment key back, please."

He reluctantly placed it in her hand. "It doesn't have to end this way, Sasha."

"Too late, Blake. It's already over." She glanced from one man to the other through her gathering tears. "I want nothing more to do with either of you." Knowing she was seconds away from losing the last of her control, she added, "Now, feel free to resume your shouting match. But I would appreciate you taking it elsewhere. I have no desire to listen to anything more that either of you have to say."

Her heart breaking, Sasha entered her apartment and closed the door behind her. Shaking uncontrollably, she leaned back against it, then covering her face with her hands, sank to the floor as she released the torrent of tears she'd been holding at bay. How could she have been so stupid? Why hadn't she been able to see past Blake's handsome face and charming smile to the coldhearted man inside?

She should have known there was more behind his excuse than just wanting to get to know her better. He'd had ample opportunity in the four years she'd worked at Dakota Fortune to strike up an acquaintance with her. But he hadn't bothered to look her way. At least, not until Creed had asked her to help him keep the fortune-hunting women in search of a great catch at arm's length by accompanying him to various events.

That should have been her first clue. But she hadn't wanted to believe that the man she'd loved from the moment she'd first laid eyes on him had only noticed her because he thought she was involved with his brother. That was the reason behind his continual questions about her relationship with Creed. He hadn't wanted to make sure he wasn't treading on another man's turf. Blake had been trying to ascertain whether he was seducing the right woman.

Her breath caught and a fresh wave of pain coursed through her. How pathetic she must have seemed to Blake when she'd told him that she'd saved herself because in her mind no man had ever measured up to him.

Hauling herself to her feet, she walked into the bedroom, but when she looked at the bed, she backpedaled and went into the kitchen. Her gaze automatically landed on the counter where he'd made love to her and, rushing from the room, she prowled her apartment in search of something, anything, that didn't remind her of Blake. But his memory was everywhere—holding her, kissing her, making love to her.

When she finally collapsed on the bed, Sasha hugged one of the pillows to her chest as she tried to stop the pain inside of her. How could a heart still beat when it was so badly broken? When it hurt so much? And how was she ever going to survive waking up in the morning without having him in her life?

Seated on a stool at the end of the bar in the lounge at the Belle of Fortune, Blake motioned for the bartender to bring him another round. He'd never been much of a drinker, but in the past few days, he figured he'd consumed enough beer to finance another team of Clydesdales and the wagon they pulled. But no matter how much he drank, Blake couldn't wash away the image of Sasha's tears or her shattered expression when she'd told him she never wanted to see him again.

He'd been a fool to even think of seducing her to get back at Creed in the first place. Then, when she'd repeatedly told him there was nothing romantic about her friendship with his brother, he'd stubbornly held to his plan and taken her to bed. And if that wasn't enough to qualify him for jerk of the year, he'd done the very thing he'd promised Sasha he would never do. He'd hurt her.

But a good case of guilty conscience wasn't his only problem. He still wasn't ready to put a name to what he felt for Sasha, but she had come to mean a great deal to him and he was hurting, too.

How could everything have gotten so far out of control? And what the hell could he do to make things right?

"Why don't you give her a call?" Sam asked, sitting another foaming mug of the amber liquid in front of Blake.

He hadn't told any of his employees about his breakup with Sasha. For one thing, it was none of their business. And for another, as long as he kept it quiet, he could fool himself into believing they weren't really through.

Glancing up from his beer, Blake gave the bartender a warning look. "Leave it alone, Sam."

Sam whistled low. "It's as bad as all that, huh?"

Blake stared at the middle-aged man behind the bar. He'd known Sam a long time and, although they'd never been close friends, he knew he could talk to the bartender and whatever was said would go no further.

"I doubt that she'd talk to me," Blake said, taking a swig of his beer.

Sam gave him an understanding nod. "Women

can be that way sometimes." He chuckled. "But if we grovel enough, they eventually come around."

"Not this time," Blake said, shaking his head. "I screwed up big time."

It was the first time he'd admitted, even to himself, that he'd made a huge error in judgment. But if confession was good for the soul, he hadn't felt it yet. He was still as miserable as hell.

"I don't know what you did, but it can't be all that bad. Have you tried sending her flowers?" Sam asked as he wiped away a spot from the top of the polished bar. "When I get in trouble with my wife, I can usually wiggle out of it with a dozen roses."

Blake grunted. "I could send her enough flowers to decorate every float in the Rose Bowl parade and I doubt it would make a difference."

"Damn, son, you are in trouble."

When Sam walked down the bar to wait on a customer, Blake wondered what he could possibly do to straighten out the mess he'd made of things. He supposed that he could send her flowers. Hell, he was at the point where he'd be willing to buy out a flower shop if that was what it took to get her to listen to him.

"You might try sending candy along with those flowers," Sam offered helpfully when he returned.

"I haven't seen a women yet who can resist a box of chocolates."

Blake nodded as he drained the last of his beer and stood up to remove his wallet from his suit coat. He tossed a hundred-dollar bill on the bar in front of the man. "Thanks, Sam."

"Hey, what's that for?" Sam asked, looking confused. "You're the boss. You don't pay for drinks."

"That's for the advice," Blake said as he left the bar.

He doubted that sending flowers and candy would be enough to mend the rift he'd created between himself and Sasha, but he was going to give it a shot. He wanted her back in his life, back in his arms and back in his bed. And come hell or high water, he wasn't going to give up until he had all three.

Nine

Sasha's stomach churned when she opened the newspaper to see the picture of her and Blake kissing. "Not again," she moaned.

After the nightmare of having her association with the Fortune brothers reported in print, she'd made a habit of checking the gossip column each morning to reassure herself the reporter had lost interest in her. But seeing the same picture next to a caption reading, "Sasha Kilgore rids herself of another Fortune, but will she gain a son…or daughter?" made her feel physically ill.

Where on earth had the columnist come up with

her information? And why hadn't she verified the facts before reporting something so blatantly false?

Sasha wasn't surprised by the report that she and Blake were no longer a couple. Anyone who cared to take notice would figure that out when they were no longer seen together. But why had the reporter added that she might be pregnant?

"Please let me be having a nightmare," she mumbled, running for the bathroom to be sick.

A few minutes later, as she splashed cold water on her face, the telephone rang and she had to abandon the hope that she'd wake up to find it had all been a dream. "Hello?"

"Sasha, don't hang up," Creed said as soon as she answered.

"I thought I told you our friendship is over." Could her day get any worse?

"I just wanted to make sure you're all right." Something in his voice told her that he'd read the morning paper.

"You saw it, didn't you?"

"I couldn't miss it." He paused. "Is it true? Did that bastard make you pregnant?"

She'd been wrong. Instead of getting worse, her day had just hit rock bottom. "No, Creed. I'm not pregnant. But thank you for reminding me that everyone in western South Dakota thinks that I am."

He cleared his throat. "Are you absolutely certain?"

"I'm positive," she said through clenched teeth. Short of assuring him of the regularity of her monthly cycle, she didn't know how to make it any clearer. The sound of the doorbell was a welcome excuse to end the call. "I have to go, Creed."

"Take care, Sasha," he said, sounding as if he'd like to say more.

She broke the connection without saying goodbye, tossed the cordless phone onto the bed and went to see who was at the door.

"Sasha Kilgore?"

"Yes," she said, eyeing the bouquet of purple hyacinth in a cut-glass vase the man held.

"These are for you." He removed a clipboard from beneath his arm. "Sign here, please."

She shook her head. "Not until I know who they're from."

Smiling, the man glanced at the paper on the clipboard. "It says here that Mr. Fortune down in Deadwood placed the order."

Sasha reached to close the door. "I don't want them."

The man looked thunderstruck. "You don't?"

"No."

"What am I supposed to do with them?" he

asked, frowning. "My boss will have my hide if I take them back to the shop."

Sasha sighed and hastily scrawling her name on the delivery slip, took the flowers from him and closed the door. After what he'd done to her, the way he'd used her, Blake thought he could atone by sending her a handful of flowers?

"I don't think so," she said as she walked straight into the utility room to throw the flowers in the trash can.

But the sight of a small envelope on a clear pick in the middle of the bouquet stopped her. A part of her wanted to read the card, to see what message Blake had included with the beautiful hyacinth and savor any connection, no matter small, with the man she loved. Another, more cautious part of her prevented her from doing it. It would only deepen her sorrow and remind her of how miserable she was.

"As if I don't already know," she said, shaking her head.

Leaving the card on the pick, she walked back into the living room and placed the flowers on a table at the end of her couch. She started to walk away, but then, as if in a trance, she sat down and spent the rest of the morning staring at them.

* * *

"You've gone too far this time, Trina," Blake said through clenched teeth when his mother opened her door. More angry with her than he could ever remember, he pushed past her to enter the condo.

Trina hurriedly stepped back to keep from being run down. "Blake, darling, whatever do you mean?"

"You know damned good and well what I mean," he said, waving a copy of the morning newspaper under her nose.

She didn't bother pretending she didn't know what he was talking about. But shaking her head, she gave him a practiced smile. "This really isn't a good time for a visit, darling. I have to go to the gym for my workout with my personal trainer." She touched her bleached blond hair with a perfectly manicured hand. "Then I have a hair and nail appointment."

"Cancel your appointments." Blake wasn't going to leave until he'd put a stop to her vicious game of revenge once and for all.

"Blake, really—"

"Leaking information to the media about Case, Max and Eliza was bad enough, but your own son?" He took a step toward her. "That's going a little far, even for you."

"What makes you think that I'm responsible for the things reported in the newspaper?" She had the audacity to look hurt by his accusations. But Blake knew his mother all too well.

He'd already given her a stern warning about her use of the media to make trouble for the family and she'd denied any involvement. And although he hadn't been entirely convinced, Blake had dismissed the matter. He'd regretted that Eliza and Max had been hurt by having their secrets revealed in print. However, he couldn't have cared less about the effect his mother's activities had on Case.

But now it appeared that he and Sasha had fallen victim to Trina's game of vengeance against the Fortune family, and Blake had every intention of putting an end to it.

"Cut the crap, Trina. We both know that you and this gossip monger attend the same exercise classes," he said, thumping the paper with a flick of his finger. "What I'd like to know is where you're getting your information about the Fortunes."

Abandoning all pretense, a bitter expression replaced his mother's look of feigned bewilderment. "It doesn't matter where I get my information, I'm making Nash Fortune's life as miserable as he's made mine and that's all I care about."

"How the hell do you figure you're making Dad

miserable when it's not the details of his private life you're putting out there for all the world to see?" Blake shoved the newspaper into her hands. "This is my name and that of an innocent woman you're dragging through the mud this time."

"I want everyone in Sioux Falls to know what a fine, upstanding family the Fortunes really are," she said sarcastically. "And why I had the good sense to get out of it."

"Oh, that's rich, Trina." Blake laughed humorlessly. "Everyone from here to St. Louis and back knows that Dad pitched you out with nothing but you're prenup when he found out you were having a series of affairs."

"Nash Fortune ruined my life," she snarled, the angry lines that would normally appear around her mouth nonexistent from her latest BOTOX injection. "He owes me for everything he's put me through."

"No, Trina, *you* were the one who ruined your life, not Dad." Blake shook his head. "And believe me, your prenuptial agreement guaranteed that you were well compensated for anything, real or imagined, that he put you through."

"It wasn't enough," she shrieked. "It will never be enough. I'm having to face the world alone because of him."

"Whatever," Blake said, realizing there was no reasoning with her where his father was concerned. Nor did he remind her that she wasn't entirely alone. She had two grown children. But then, she'd never had more than a passing interest in anything about him or Skylar. "You will cease and desist your efforts to ruin the rest of us through this gossip column."

"I haven't told my friend anything that wasn't absolutely true," she said haughtily.

"That's bull and we both know it." He took a deep breath. "Sasha has never been, nor will she ever be a social climber. And she's not pregnant."

A sudden thought caused his gut to tighten. He'd been careful to make sure they were protected, but there had been that one time in her kitchen when he'd been so hot for her that he hadn't taken the time to use a condom. The chances were remote that he'd gotten her pregnant, but still there was the possibility.

"Are you certain?" Trina asked, giving him a sly look.

"Relatively," he said, remembering that Sasha had a period shortly after the careless incident.

His mother frowned. "But Ivy said—" The moment she spoke the name of the Fortunes' chef, Trina clamped her mouth shut.

"So she's the one supplying you with information about us," Blake said, not at all surprised.

Before his father had divorced Trina, she and Ivy had become good friends. At least, as good friends as two troublemakers could be. Apparently, they'd stayed in touch and Ivy was feeding snippets of overheard conversations to Trina.

"I don't give a damn what she tells you—you will stop reporting our every move to this sleazy reporter," Blake said, pointing to the newspaper. "Either that, or I'll sever all ties with you and you really will be alone in the world."

Before Trina could argue the point further, Blake walked out of the condo and climbed into his sports car. How could anyone be so set on revenge that it became all-consuming?

As he started the engine and backed from the parking slot, he felt as if tiny leprechauns in spiked shoes were dancing an Irish jig inside his stomach. But then, that was nothing new. He could never remember a time that a visit with his mother hadn't made him feel that way.

Steering the car out of the parking lot, Blake set the cruise control as he headed across town to the florist to order more flowers for Sasha. He wondered if she'd seen the gossip column and how she'd reacted to it. She'd been extremely upset by the first report, but this story was far worse, and no doubt, caused her an even greater amount of distress.

The knot in his stomach tightened to an unbearable ache. It wasn't any wonder she wanted nothing more to do with his family. Her association with them had brought her nothing but pain and heartache. And he hated that she'd been caught up in the vengeful games he and his family insisted on playing with each other.

As the realization of what he'd done to her sank in, he took a deep breath against the guilt weighing heavily on his shoulders. His need to even the score with Creed was directly responsible for her recent unhappiness.

Disgusted with himself, he came to the conclusion that he was no better than Trina. His mother had wasted a huge amount of her life trying to get even with his father for the mistakes *she'd* made, not Nash. And Blake was just as guilty of holding a grudge against his brothers, Case and Creed, for reasons beyond their control.

Blake supposed that to one degree or another, all families had their rivalries. But the Fortune brothers had let theirs get dangerously out of control. Case and Creed had always resented Blake, probably because they'd never liked his mother. And for as long as Blake could remember, Trina had been extremely vocal about the differences she felt Nash made between his two older sons and Blake. After years of listening to her harp on the subject, it was no wonder his resentment had built to choking proportions.

But he couldn't lay all the blame at Trina's doorstep. He'd spent more time and energy than he cared to admit nurturing the hard feelings he had for his brothers…and where had it gotten him? Absolutely nowhere. It had been an enormous waste of his energy and spirit and it was past time he let it go.

Besides, he had another, even stronger emotion replacing his resentment and hostilities. It scared the living hell out of him to acknowledge it and God only knew he'd fought valiantly against it, but somewhere between his decision to seduce her and the confrontation with Creed at her apartment, he'd fallen in love with Sasha.

He shook his head as he parked his car in the florist's parking lot. His mind set on what he wanted, he walked into the flower shop. As soon as he arranged for several more bouquets to be delivered to her, he fully intended to go over to her place and if he had to, wear out the knees on his khakis begging her to forgive him and take him back.

* * *

As Blake left the florist, his cell phone rang and when he answered it, he was startled by the sound of his step-sister's frantic voice. "Blake, have you seen my mother?"

A year younger than his sister, Skylar, Maya Blackstone had been raised with the Fortune children when Nash had hired Patricia to take care of them after his divorce from Trina. Blake had always liked Maya well enough, but she'd never seemed to feel as if she were part of the Fortune family. All things considered, Blake wasn't entirely sure he blamed her.

"What's wrong, Maya?"

"We can't find Mother." Her voice shook and he knew she was trying her best not to cry.

"Dad doesn't know where she is?" he asked, getting into his car. It wasn't often that his step-mother left the house without Nash, and when she did, she always let him know where she was going and when she'd return.

"No and he's in a total panic. He had me called out of the class I was teaching to see if I'd seen her."

"Are you still at school?" he asked, steering the little sports car toward Fortune Estate.

"Yes. I have another class to teach and no one to cover for me."

"I'm only about fifteen minutes away," he assured her. "I'll stop by the estate and see if I can find out what's going on."

"Please call me back and let me know what you find out," she begged.

"I will, Maya."

Several minutes later, when Blake drove up the circular drive in front of the estate and got out of the car to climb the steps of the front veranda, Nash barreled out of the front door to meet him. "Have you seen Patricia?"

"No." He'd never seen Nash Fortune panic over anything, but he was certainly on the verge of it now. "What's going on, Dad?"

"I don't know," Nash said, his gaze riveted on the driveway as if he was willing his wife to come home. "It looks like she's left me, son. And I don't know why."

Blake couldn't believe it. Patricia was as devoted to his father as Nash was to her.

"Did you argue?" he asked, trying to make sense of it all.

Nash shook his head. "You know we never disagree."

It was true. In the thirteen years they'd been married, Blake couldn't remember a single time they'd had a difference of opinion about anything.

"Are you sure she's left you? Maybe she's just gone to run some errands or decided to go shopping," Blake offered, hoping that was the case.

"She took some of her clothes," Nash said dejectedly. He lowered himself onto one of the decorative wrought-iron chairs on the veranda. "What am I going to do, son?"

"I don't know, Dad." He knew exactly how his father felt. Since Sasha had told him she never wanted to see him again, it had been the worst four days of his life.

"If I knew what I'd done to upset her, I'd make it right," Nash said, propping his forearms on his bent knees. He stared down at his loosely clasped hands hanging between his knees. "But I don't have the slightest notion where she went."

Blake didn't know where to tell his father to start looking, but he did know where his woman was and he wasn't going to waste any more time finding her to straighten things out between them. "Dad, I'll keep my eyes open and if see her, I'll let you know."

Nash raised sad eyes and the desolation in his gaze shocked Blake. "Please do, son. I don't know if I can survive without her."

Blake knew where his father was coming from and he wasn't about to waste another precious minute getting to the woman he loved. "I have to leave, Dad. But keep me posted if you find out anything."

"I will."

"Oh, Dad, you might want to start looking for another chef," Blake said, remembering his conversation with Trina.

"Why?"

"Ivy's the one responsible for spreading gossip to Trina about everything that's going on around here."

"I'll fire her immediately," Nash said coldly. "Her mentioning Trina all the time might be behind Patricia leaving."

Blake knew there had to be more behind his stepmother walking out on the man she loved, but he couldn't think about that now. He had to get to Sasha.

Leaving his father sitting on the veranda, staring down the driveway as he drove away, Blake called Maya to tell her what he'd found out, then ending the call, he headed back into Sioux Falls.

He felt sorry for Nash and the wretchedness he was feeling. Blake had felt the same way ever since Sasha had told him she never wanted to see him again.

But that was about to change. He was going over to her apartment and he wasn't leaving until he'd made things right with her.

* * *

Closing her apartment door, Sasha turned to search for a place to set the latest bouquet of flowers that had just been delivered. She was rapidly running out of flat surfaces to put them on and would soon have to start setting them on the floor.

After the bouquet of purple hyacinth had arrived that morning, every hour on the hour, the delivery-man was back at her door with another arrangement. There were bouquets of a variety of flowers and in every color imaginable. And tucked into each one was a card with her name scrawled across the envelope in Blake's handwriting. She hadn't opened any of them, but it was getting more difficult with each delivery to resist the temptation of finding out what Blake had written.

Placing the vase of yellow jonquils she held on top of the television, she glanced at the clock on the DVD player. It was getting close to the time for shops to close and, hopefully, it would be the last delivery she received for the day.

But when the doorbell rang, her shoulders slumped. "There couldn't possibly be any flowers left in Sioux Falls," she muttered as she walked to the door. "They're all here in my apartment.

Swinging the door open, she started to tell the deliveryman to start taking them to the local hospital, but the words froze in her throat and her heart pounded so hard against her ribs she was surprised it wasn't audible. Instead of another floral arrangement, Blake Fortune was standing at her door holding a single long-stemmed red rose in full bloom.

Ten

"Go away," Sasha said, reaching to close the door.

Blake looked so good it brought tears to her eyes and she felt as if her heart would break all over again. Even after all that he'd done, she loved him more than anything. But she wasn't fool enough to let him into her life again. Not if she wanted to maintain what little sanity she had left.

"Wait, sweetheart," he said, placing his hand on the surface of the door to hold it open. "I have something I need to tell you."

"I don't want to hear it," she said, shoving at the

door. She was no match for his superior strength, but that didn't keep her from trying to slam the door in his face. "As far as I'm concerned, we have nothing left to say to each other."

"Come on, Sasha. Give me ten minutes."

"No."

"Please?"

"No." She stubbornly pushed at the door. He didn't seem to be expending a whole lot of energy to hold the door open, but she was quickly becoming exhausted from her efforts. "Now, please remove your hand and go away."

Shrugging, he replaced his hand with his shoulder. "Is that more to your liking?"

She shook her head. "You haven't gone away."

"You might as well let me in, sweetheart."

The look he gave her caused her chest to tighten with emotion and she doubled her efforts to shut the door. "What part of 'go away' don't you understand?"

"I'm not going anywhere until you listen to me," he said patiently.

"There's nothing you have to say that I want to hear."

Why was he being so darned persistent? Why couldn't he leave her alone and let her try to put the shattered pieces of her life back together?

Apparently tired of leaning against the door, he used his shoulder to push it open a little farther and entered her apartment. "You might not want to hear it, but I'm going to tell you anyway."

"Haven't you said enough already?" she asked, glaring at him as she closed the door.

He twirled the long-stemmed rose between his fingers as he walked over to inspect the vase of purple hyacinth. "Did you know that the type and color of a bouquet sends a message?"

"I've heard that, but I have no idea what each flower means and right now, I don't really care." Her heart was breaking and he wanted to discuss the flowers he'd sent her?

"You didn't read the cards that accompanied the arrangements, did you?" he asked as he plucked the small envelope from the bouquet.

"No." She wasn't about to tell him that the hardest thing she'd ever done was to resist reading the messages he'd included.

"That's a shame," he said, removing the card from the envelope. "I wrote down the meaning of each one on the cards."

"Are you going to tell me why you're here or give me a lesson in flowers?" The longer he stayed, the harder it would be for her when she had to watch him leave.

"The purple hyacinth says, 'I'm sorry, please forgive me,'" he said as if she hadn't spoken.

"That's nice, but we both know that forgiving you is going to be impossible for me to do." Tears threatened, but she blinked them away. She had more pride than to allow him to see how much she was still hurting.

"Are you certain of that?"

She couldn't believe he had the nerve to ask. "Yes."

He didn't turn to face her, nor did he comment further. Instead, he reached for the card tucked in a beautiful Boston fern. "Did you know that the fern signifies sincerity?"

"Oh, really?" She didn't even try to keep the bitterness from her voice. "I wasn't aware that you knew the meaning of the word."

Instead of responding to her remark, he walked over to another arrangement. "Pink roses ask that you please believe me."

"Why should I believe you or anything you say? I believed you when you said you'd never do anything to hurt me." She shook her head at her own foolishness. "But we both know how that turned out."

He still hadn't looked at her and the only indication that he'd heard her was in the slight stiffening of his shoulders. "Red carnations say that my heart aches for you," he said, moving on to the vase on her coffee table.

"Blake, stop…this," she said, hating the hitch in her voice. The more she listened to him, the closer she got to dissolving into a pool of tears. "P-please, if you have any compassion, you'll leave me alone."

"A bouquet of primrose means I can't live without you," he said, ignoring her passionate plea.

Why was he doing this to her? Hadn't he hurt her enough with his empty promises and insincerity? What made him think that by telling her the meanings behind the flowers he'd convince her to believe him now?

He touched the planter of white violets next to the primrose and stared at it for endless seconds before he spoke again. "These ask that you take a chance on happiness with me."

His relentless continuation was slowly destroying her. "P-please, don't—"

He hesitated a moment as if he was going to face her, then moved on to the final bouquet she'd placed on the television only moments before his arrival. "The yellow jonquils ask that you love me," he said quietly.

Sasha felt as if her heart broke all over again. How could he ask that of her?

"I—I did…love you," she said brokenly. "B-but I can't…" She shook her head. "W-won't put myself…in that position…again."

"Why not?" he asked, his back still to her.

He had to ask? Was he so self-absorbed that he couldn't see how much he'd hurt her?

"B-because I can't let you…hurt me again, Blake," she said, unable to keep her voice from cracking. "I—I can't…go through that again."

Finally turning to face her, he touched a velvety petal on the rose in his hand. "Do you know what a single red rose means, Sasha?"

She swallowed hard as she shook her head.

Walking over to stand in front of her, Blake handed her the long-stemmed rose, then held her hand between both of his. "It means I love you, sweetheart."

His warm touch was heaven and hell rolled into one. "D-don't," she said, forcing the word passed her tight throat. She fixed her gaze on the perfect rose to keep from looking at him. If she did, she knew for certain she'd be lost. "Y-you don't have any idea…what love is, Blake."

He was silent for a long moment. "That was probably true a month ago," he admitted, surprising her. "But that was before you."

Unable to believe him, the rose fell to the floor

as she pulled away. "If you loved me, why did you tell Creed that you'd won?" She shook her head. "Do you have any idea how that made me feel? To know that the man I love with all my heart was only using me in an attempt to get back at his brother?"

He bent down to pick up the rose. When he straightened, he nodded. "I know I've hurt you terribly, Sasha. And if I could, I'd turn back time and do things a lot different."

"Why don't you just come out and say it, Blake?" she asked, drawing on anger born from the emotional pain that seeing him again had caused. "If you hadn't thought I was involved with Creed, you wouldn't have been interested in me in the first place. You would have continued to come and go at Dakota Fortune without giving me a second glance."

They both knew what she said was true and he had the good graces not to refute it.

But when he raised his eyes to look directly at her, the regret in their blue depths stole her breath. "Unfortunately, you're probably right, sweetheart. But it didn't take me long to see how special you truly are."

"Was that before or after I gave you my virginity?" she asked, unable to stop herself.

He took a deep breath and the truth in his gaze

caused her heart to skip a beat. "I don't ever want you to doubt how much that meant to me. Just knowing that you'd always wanted me humbles me in ways you could never imagine."

"Then why…did you tell Creed—"

"That I figured out the two of you weren't involved when I took your virginity?" he finished for her. When she nodded, he shook his head. "Because I was a stupid, selfish bastard, who spoke in the heat of the moment when he should have kept his mouth shut."

"How many innocent victims are you and your brothers going to destroy before you stop this senseless feud, Blake? How far are you willing to go with your game of revenge?" When he took a step toward her, she shook her head. "Please don't."

But as was his custom, Blake ignored her and took her into his arms. "It stops right now, sweetheart."

The feel of his arms around her once again was her undoing and, burying her face in his chest, she gave into the tears she could no longer hold in check. There was no use pretending. No matter what he'd done, she still loved him, would always love him. But could she ever trust him?

"It's okay, Sasha," he said, tightening his hold around her. "You're more important to me than anything else in the world and I swear if you'll give us—give me—another chance, I'll never do anything to hurt you or make you unhappy ever again." His voice grew husky with emotion. "I want nothing more than to spend the rest of my life loving you." He threaded his fingers through her hair and tilted her head so that their gazes met. "I want to make love to you every night and wake up with you in my arms each morning for as long as I live."

"Wh-what are you saying?" she asked, afraid to believe.

The sincerity in his smile and the truth in his eyes couldn't be denied. "I want it all. I want you to move to Deadwood with me. I want us to run our casinos and raise babies together. And when they grow up and leave home, I want us to grow old together."

Lowering his head, he gave her a kiss so soft, so tender, there was no doubt left in her mind that he meant what he said.

When he raised his head there was a suspicious sheen of moisture in his eyes. "I love you, Sasha Kilgore. Can you find it in your heart to forgive me and do me the honor of becoming Mrs. Blake Fortune?"

Her tears fell anew, but this time they were tears

of joy. "Oh, Blake. Do you really mean it? Do you really want all those things?"

"Sweetheart, I've never wanted anything more in my entire life," he said without a moment's hesitation. "Will you marry me?"

"I love you, too, darling." Throwing her arms around his neck, she gazed up at the man she loved with all of her heart and soul. "Yes, I'll marry you."

He kissed her then and the love in that single kiss was more pure and beautiful than she'd ever thought possible.

"You've just made me the happiest man alive, Sasha." His smile caused her chest to fill with such intense emotion it took her breath. "And I intend to spend the rest of my days seeing that you never regret loving me."

"I could never regret loving you, Blake. I gave you my heart when I was fifteen and never took it back."

He shook his head. "And I never intend to let it go."

As they gazed lovingly at each other, she hesitated a moment before she said, "Blake, I want you to do something before we get married."

"Name it, sweetheart, and I'll see that it's taken care of."

"It's not for me," she said softly. "It's for you."

He looked confused. "You want something for me?"

She nodded. "I want you to make peace with your brothers."

To her surprise, he nodded. "I've seen what holding grudges and trying to even scores has done to my family." He touched her cheek. "And what it almost cost me." He gave her a tender kiss. "Revenge for something, whether real or imagined, isn't worth losing the one you love."

Sasha hugged him. "I love you, Blake Fortune."

"And I love you, sweetheart. For as long as I live."

* * * * *

Don't miss the next DAKOTA FORTUNES *book,*
EXPECTING A FORTUNE by Jan Colley,
available in May from Silhouette Desire.

Set in darkness beyond the ordinary world.
Passionate tales of life and death.
With characters' lives ruled by laws the everyday
world can't begin to imagine.

n✹cturne

It's time to discover the Raintree trilogy....

New York Times bestselling author
LINDA HOWARD
brings you the dramatic first book
RAINTREE: INFERNO

The Ansara Wizards are rising and the
Raintree clan must rejoin the battle against
their foes, testing their powers, relationships
and forcing upon them lives they never
could have imagined before....

Turn the page for a sneak preview
of the captivating first book
in the Raintree trilogy,
RAINTREE: INFERNO by LINDA HOWARD
On sale April 2.

Dante Raintree stood with his arms crossed as he watched the woman on the monitor. The image was in black and white to better show details; color distracted the brain. He focused on her hands, watching every move she made, but what struck him most was how uncommonly *still* she was. She didn't fidget or play with her chips, or look around at the other players. She peeked once at her down card, then didn't touch it again, signaling for another hit by tapping a fingernail on the table. Just because she didn't seem to be paying attention to the other players, though, didn't mean she was as unaware as she seemed.

"What's her name?" Dante asked.

"Lorna Clay," replied his chief of security, Al Rayburn.

"At first I thought she was counting, but she doesn't pay enough attention."

"She's paying attention, all right," Dante murmured. "You just don't see her doing it." A card counter had to remember every card played. Supposedly counting cards was impossible with the number of decks used by the casinos, but there were those rare individuals who could calculate the odds even with multiple decks.

"I thought that, too," said Al. "But look at this piece of tape coming up. Someone she knows comes up to her and speaks, she looks around and starts chatting, completely misses the play of the people to her left—and doesn't look around even when the deal comes back to her, just taps that finger. And damn if she didn't win. Again."

Dante watched the tape, rewound it, watched it again. Then he watched it a third time. There had to be something he was missing, because he couldn't pick out a single giveaway.

"If she's cheating," Al said with something like respect, "she's the best I've ever seen."

"What does your gut say?"

Al scratched the side of his jaw, considering. Finally, he said, "If she isn't cheating, she's the luckiest person walking. She wins. Week in, week out, she wins. Never a huge amount, but I ran the numbers and she's into us for about five grand a week. Hell, boss, on her way out of the casino she'll stop by a slot machine, feed a dollar in and walk away with at least fifty. It's never the same machine, either. I've had her watched, I've had her followed, I've even looked for the same faces in the casino every time she's in here, and I can't find a common denominator."

"Is she here now?"

"She came in about half an hour ago. She's playing blackjack, as usual.

"Bring her to my office," Dante said, making a swift decision. "Don't make a scene."

"Got it," said Al, turning on his heel and leaving the security center.

Dante left, too, going up to his office. His face was calm. Normally he would leave it to Al to deal with a cheater, but he was curious. How was she doing it? There were a lot of bad cheaters, a few good ones, and every so often one would come along who was the stuff of which legends were made: the cheater who didn't get caught, even when people were alert and the camera was on him—or, in this case, her.

It was possible to simply be lucky, as most people understood luck. Chance could turn a habitual loser into a big-time winner. Casinos, in fact, thrived on that hope. But luck itself wasn't habitual, and he knew that what passed for luck was often something else: cheating. And there was the other kind of luck, the kind he himself possessed, but it depended not on chance but on who and what he was. He knew it was an innate power and not Dame Fortune's erratic smile. Since power like his was rare, the odds made it likely the woman he'd been watching was merely a very clever cheat.

Her skill could provide her with a very good living, he thought, doing some swift calculations in his head. Five grand a week equaled $260,000 a year, and that was just from his casino. She probably hit them all, careful to keep the numbers relatively low so she stayed under the radar.

He wondered how long she'd been taking him, how long she'd been winning a little here, a little there, before Al noticed.

The curtains were open on the wall-to-wall window in his office, giving the impression, when one first opened the door, of stepping out onto a covered balcony. The glazed window faced west, so he could catch the sunsets. The sun was low now, the sky painted in purple and gold. At his home in the mountains, most of the windows faced east, affording him views of the sunrise. Something in him needed both the greeting and the goodbye of the sun. He'd always been drawn to sunlight, maybe because fire was his element to call, to control.

He checked his internal time: four minutes until sundown. Without checking the sunrise tables every day, he knew exactly when the sun would slide behind the mountains. He didn't own an alarm clock. He didn't need one. He was so acutely attuned to the sun's position that he had only to check within himself to know the time. As for waking at a particular time, he was one of those people who could tell himself to wake at a certain time, and he did. That talent had nothing to do with being Raintree, so he didn't have to hide it; a lot of perfectly ordinary people had the same ability.

He had other talents and abilities, however, that did require careful shielding. The long days of summer instilled in him an almost sexual high, when he could feel contained power buzzing just beneath his skin. He had to be doubly careful not to cause candles to leap into flame just by his presence, or to start wildfires with a glance in the dry-as-tinder brush. He loved Reno; he didn't want to burn it down. He just felt so damn *alive* with all the sunshine pouring down that he wanted to let the energy pour through him instead of holding it inside.

This must be how his brother Gideon felt while pulling lightning, all that hot power searing through his muscles, his veins. They had this in common, the connection with raw power. All the members of the far-flung Raintree clan had some power, some heightened ability, but only members of the royal family could channel and control the earth's natural energies.

Dante wasn't just of the royal family, he was the Dranir, the leader of the entire clan. "Dranir" was synonymous with king, but the position he held wasn't ceremonial, it was one of sheer power. He was the oldest son of the previous Dranir, but he would have been passed over for the position if he hadn't also inherited the power to hold it.

Behind him came Al's distinctive knock on the door. The outer office was empty, Dante's secretary having gone home hours before. "Come in," he called, not turning from his view of the sunset.

The door opened, and Al said, "Mr. Raintree, this is Lorna Clay."

Dante turned and looked at the woman, all his

senses on alert. The first thing he noticed was the vibrant color of her hair, a rich, dark red that encompassed a multitude of shades from copper to burgundy. The warm amber light danced along the iridescent strands, and he felt a hard tug of sheer lust in his gut. Looking at her hair was almost like looking at fire, and he had the same reaction.

The second thing he noticed was that she was spitting mad.

nocturne™

IT'S TIME TO DISCOVER
THE RAINTREE TRILOGY...

There have always been those among us
who are more than human...

Don't miss the dramatic first book by

New York Times bestselling author

LINDA
HOWARD

RAINTREE:
Inferno

On sale May.

Raintree: Haunted by Linda Winstead Jones
Available June.

Raintree: Sanctuary by Beverly Barton
Available July.

SNLHIBC

Silhouette®
Romantic
SUSPENSE

**Sparked by Danger,
Fueled by Passion.**

*This month and every month look for
four new heart-racing romances
set against a backdrop of suspense!*

REQUEST YOUR FREE BOOKS!

2 FREE NOVELS PLUS 2 FREE GIFTS!

Passionate, Powerful, Provocative!

SDES07

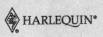